THE BATMAN AND THE BALLERINA

Readers are encouraged to go to www.MissionPointPress. com to contact the author or to find information on how to buy this book in bulk at a discounted rate.

Published by Mission Point Press
2554 Chandler Rd.
Traverse City, MI 49686
(231) 421-9513
www.MissionPointPress.com

Cover design by Heather Lee Shaw.
Cover illustrations by Tajín Robles.

ISBN: 978-1-943995-91-2
Library of Congress Control Number: 2018958671

Printed in the United States of America.

THE **BATMAN**
AND THE **BALLERINA**

DEAN FELDPAUSCH

MISSION POINT PRESS

CONTENTS

INTRODUCTION

In the winter of 2017 I became interested in a gentleman named Clem Sohn. Clem was an aviator and skydiver who was renowned throughout the United States and Europe in the 1930's. He developed wings of his own design, which he used to glide horizontally in the sky. This was most unusual at this time in history and his adoring fans dubbed Clem "Batman".

My interest in him was born from the fact that Clem is a blood relation to my wife Marcia; a second cousin to be exact. My wife's grandfather, John Kramer, was the brother of Rosalia (Kramer) Sohn, who was Clem's mother. I had an opportunity to review old family black-and-white photo albums, which revealed a limited number of pictures of this American hero from his childhood to adulthood. I also found some pictures of old postcards and newspaper articles regarding his triumphs as a Batman. Among these family keepsakes were some writings that contained a little information about Clem's life. One such writing captured my interest because it mentioned a strange circumstance between Clem and famed English ballerina Margot Fonteyn.

Clem was a professional aviator and was perhaps the best in the world at what he did. Margot was also a consummate professional and perhaps the best in the world on the dance stage. Margot wrote in her autobiography about receiving a bouquet of flowers and a note from Clem after one of her performances just a few days before he perished in France in 1937. With this nugget of information I performed research into both of their life's stories to determine the extent of their relationship. There was virtually no information available. Scouring through ancestry information, newspaper articles, census records, ship manifests, and anything else I could find, I turned up little information. However, during the course of this information gathering I developed a love for both of these individuals and I decided I wanted to write a fictional account about them in a way that would endear them to the world in the way that I had become endeared to them.

The Batman and the Ballerina is a fiction work based on the lives of Clem Sohn and Margot Fonteyn. Actual names of people and places have been used for the sake of authenticity. However, this story has been dramatized and may be somewhat different than how these events actually occurred. No claim is made to the accuracy of the incidents depicted in this novel.

Much of this book is based on actual facts about the lives of Clem and Margot. Much is also based on circumstances, which I strongly believe could have occurred between the lives of these two amazing individuals. It is my sincere hope that you will be entertained by their story as I've imagined it could have been

THE BATMAN AND THE BALLERINA

PERIWINKLE BOUQUET

It was about ten o'clock in the morning on April 25, 1987. I remember that day well: It was a Saturday, and unusually warm. I worked for the *Clinton County News* as a beat reporter. It wasn't exactly my dream job. I'd graduated from Michigan State University a year prior with a degree in journalism, and had aspired to work for a news outlet with a much greater circulation than some small mid-Michigan paper. I wasn't at the top of my class, so I had to settle for starting out small. My editor assigned me to cover a ceremony that was taking place later that day at the Fowler cemetery for some guy who used to parachute from airplanes about fifty years ago. His name was Clem … real impressive! If I didn't start getting any better assignments, I was going to have to decide if I really wanted to be a journalist. Several of my friends were now making big money as secretaries and teachers, while I struggled on a writer's wages.

I drove a long way from Lansing to the remote cemetery spot outside of Fowler, Michigan, to get this inconsequential story. The cemetery was an eleven-acre expanse of land on the corner of Walker and Grange roads. I wanted to get there early so that I could find Clem's headstone and take a few pictures in the morning sunlight, perhaps interview any attendees arriving prematurely. I pulled my light-blue 1978 Gremlin into a drive on the north side of the cemetery and parked in front of a rather large, dark sedan on the drive facing the road. As I approached the huge oak tree next to the north cemetery gate, I heard the squawk of a bronze grackle. I envy the freedom of travel that birds possess: I watched for a minute until the grackle finally leapt from the branch and flew off on a soft, warm current of air. I then continued down the path from the gate to the middle of the graveyard and began my search for Clem's marker.

As I made my way through the cemetery, I noticed an elderly lady sitting alone on a small, black, iron bench. She sat in the shade of a large cedar tree about twenty yards ahead of my indiscriminate search. The woman had dark-gray hair held tightly to her scalp with a black hair-tie in the back. She wore a long dress, which was periwinkle in color and trimmed with a white stitched design on her collar and the ends of her sleeves. Black stockings covered the small portions of her legs that were visible between her matching periwinkle shoes and the hem of her dress. Her dress contrasted starkly with the neon-green shirt, blue jeans, and Spartan ball cap that I wore. She didn't seem to notice my presence until I drew closer to investigate.

"Hello," I said as I approached her.

She turned slowly to me and replied with a slight smile. "Hello, young lady. I must say that I love the color of your little coupe."

This let me know that she had, in fact, been watching me. She seemed to have a slight British accent.

"Thanks," I responded. "I bought it mostly because of the color. It's not much on looks, but it gets pretty good gas mileage. Are you from this area?"

"No," she answered slowly. "I'm just visiting someone I knew a long, long time ago."

"My name is Ren Phillips," I said, privately wondering if she was here for the ceremony. "I'm pleased to meet you."

"Wren like the bird?" the woman asked.

"Well, it's pronounced like the bird, but spelled without the 'W'," I replied.

"My name is Margot. I'm here from England."

"That's rad. I've never met anyone from England before."

"Well, I've never met anyone from Fowler … except for Clem," she said, lowering her eyes.

"Clem?" I asked, interest increasing.

"Yes. Clem Sohn, the *batman*," she replied.

"Batman?"

"Oh yes, he lived long before you were born. And LIVE he did," she replied. "He's buried just over there."

My eyes found the headstone; a rather large bouquet of periwinkle flowers in a clay vase was set at the marker's base. It was a simple grave marker with a picture on the top of a cross, with wings adorning each side.

"Clements J Sohn," I read. "Born December 7, 1910. Died in France, April 25, 1937."

"Yes," said Margot. "Clem told me he didn't like his full name, 'Clements'. He was a simple chap, and just liked being called Clem. He also told me his middle name was Augustine. That 'J' is a little squiffy, if you ask me." Margot gave the letter a sharp look of disapproval.

I continued to view the stone.

"April 25th… that's today!" I exclaimed. I'd done minimal background work on this story and hadn't realized the ceremony for Clem was on the anniversary of his death.

"Yes, that's why I'm here. I wanted to be with Clem on this day," said Margot.

"It says he died in France," I noted.

"Oh yes, he did, just a few days after I last saw him," Margot said, sadness in her eyes.

We both stared at the headstone for a short period of time, thinking about the conversation we had shared up to that point.

"Why do you call him *batman*?" I asked, finally breaking the thoughtful silence.

Margot looked up at the sky as she explained. "Clem was handsome and courageous. He jumped out of airplanes in front of great, adoring crowds. He wore a special suit that he made with his mother's sewing machine, which allowed him to glide in the sky like a kestrel. When he drew near to the ground, he'd open his parachute and float ever so slowly to the earth. People at the time called him the *bat-winged man*, or *batman*." She motioned her hands to emphasize her description of gliding and floating.

"Hmm … a kestrel?" I asked.

"Oh yes, it's like your eagle here in the States," she replied. "People traveled from all over the world to see him soar among the clouds."

"That must have been something to see."

"Well," she said, looking forlorn, "I never actually got to see him perform. He told me all about it, though, and many other events in his life, too."

I felt like I had hit the jackpot. Was I actually speaking with someone who'd *known* this Clem I was assigned to write about? I wanted to learn more, so I moved toward her and sat by her feet on the cool grass.

"I'm a news reporter and would love to write about Clem. Will you tell me all about him?" I pleaded.

Margot looked thoughtful—almost suspicious—for a long moment. Then, she sighed. "I've kept his memories in my heart for so long, I guess it would do me jolly good to finally tell someone about them," she replied with a weary smile.

I placed my camera on the ground next to me, pulled my reporter's notepad out of my oversized burlap shoulder bag, and took the pencil out of the small bun I had fixed on top of my head. I began to take notes as Margot spoke and was quickly amazed by the sheer amount of information she so freely volunteered.

HANDMADE PLANES

"Clem and I got to know each other while on a ship," Margot explained. "We were both on our way to Europe. We spent a glorious week together, and got well-acquainted with each other. Clem was in his twenties, and I was just shy of my eighteenth birthday." Margot smiled dreamily, seeming to drift into a world devoid of everything around her.

She began to give her account of Clem's stories of his earliest years. She started by speaking about a particularly sad event in Clem's life. As her recollection unfolded, I could picture in my head the unique circumstances she spoke of.

"Francis … Clem …!"

Gottlieb Sohn yelled from the farmhouse door in a strong German accent.

"Come here now!"

Gottlieb was an immigrant who had traveled to America as a teenage boy. He'd been raised in a German household with a very strict father in a mid-Michigan settlement called Fowler. In his highly controlled childhood, Gottlieb was not allowed to make decisions for himself. His father was a taskmaster who demanded abundant hard work from his children on their farm. Gottlieb, now a father himself, did not raise his own sons, Francis and Clem, in this manner. At thirty-eight years of age, he did not know how to parent and had trouble relating to them. Gottlieb was a big man. He was six feet tall with a vast, bulky frame. He had large, strong hands and was physically built to handle the rigors of farm life. He was very shy and quiet as a young man. He bought a small farm north and west of Fowler just before he got married. Farming wasn't his interest, but he did not possess the confidence to decide for himself to do anything else. The farm he purchased had some small outbuildings and a livable house but was in great disrepair when he first took possession. Gottlieb was not good at mending fences or fixing buildings. He relied on the help of neighbors to improve the farm for himself, his sons, and his bride, Rosalia.

Gottlieb did not enjoy farm life as a child and found little enjoyment on his own farm as an adult. He was not at all prosperous as an agrarian on the eighty-acre parcel they called home. He simply could not occupy his mind with the day-to-day drudgery of tending livestock and working the soil. With virtually no savings, two young, audacious boys to oversee, and a sick wife, Gottlieb had grown somewhat bitter at the current state of his life. He became a quick-tempered man. His sons loved him but were in constant fear of his unpredictable wrath.

On this cold, cold Friday evening, the last day of February in 1919, Francis and Clem were working in the horse barn mucking the stalls just before sunset. Shoveling manure out of the horse barn was a task that seemed without end. Hay was shoveled into the stalls for the draft horses, Molly and Daisy, to consume, and manure was shoveled out. These draft horses provided the family with transportation as well as propulsion for the farm implements used for planting.

Francis was ten years old. He had auburn-colored hair and a medium frame. He was exceptionally strong for his age. Clem was eight and had blond hair. He, too, was wiry and strong from the man-sized work he helped Francis perform on the farm. The two were dressed in well-worn blue bib overalls and drab tee shirts beneath their thick red-plaid woolen coats. Their barn clothes were on their fifth day of wear without the benefit of laundering. They wore calf-high pull-on leather boots over woolen stockings to help keep their feet warm. They also sported cloth cotton gloves that were worn through at the fingertips and palms. The horse barn was drafty, and the cold wind blew through it. They picked and dug the frozen dung from the floor of the stalls and loaded it into a wooden wheelbarrow. This was wheeled outside onto a large manure pile, which had been accumulating since after the planting season the year before. The composted manure would be spread on the fields in early spring as fertilizer for the new crops. That meant all of this manure would be shoveled once again in the spring onto a wagon for spreading in the fields. Keeping busy was the best means of keeping their bodies and hands warm.

These two boys were adventurous by nature and daydreamed of leaving the farm and the clay dirt of Fowler to make a splash in the world. Clem loved the thought of flying. The ceiling of his bedroom was festooned with all sorts of handmade planes dangling from bale twine nailed into the horsehair plaster ceiling. He made these planes from wood and nails he found on the farm, but nothing he created could actually fly. Infrequently, an airplane would coast in the sky over the farm, the two brothers using the occasion to debate eagerly over its make and model. Airplanes had advanced at an incredible pace since the Wright Brothers made their first historic flight just fifteen years earlier. Francis dreamed of playing baseball. He was very athletic for his young age and loved to pitch a baseball during the warm months of the year.

When Gottlieb called out to his sons from the back door, the inflection in his voice told them that the matter was serious. Their mother Rosalia had been sick … very sick. Her persistent cough over the last year had grown increasingly frequent and intense. Doc Cook had visited her regularly at the farm to do what he could, but the kind doctor could not seem to come up with a healing remedy. Rosalia was confined to bed and had been for the last several winter months. Deep in his heart, Clem knew that his father's call had to do with his mom's failing health.

The boys ran into the house and removed their coats and boots. By the light of an oil lantern, they could see their father sitting at the kitchen table with his face in his hands behind a row of empty longneck Stroh's beer bottles. When Francis and Clem entered the kitchen from the mudroom, Gottlieb stood up and silently motioned them to follow him into his bedroom. When they entered, they could see their mom Rosalia lying in bed, breathing uneasily, with sunken eyes and pale skin.

The winter wind whistled as it split and twisted around the farmhouse to meet on the other side. The bedroom was ten by ten, and the walls were adorned with wallpaper filled with purple flowers resembling hydrangeas on a cream-colored background. The floor was dark tongue-in-groove wood; a large area rug protruded from under the bed, giving bare feet some relief from the hard surface. The dark wooden bed frame was made of oak and had a hand-carved bouquet of flowers on the headboard. The heavy handmade quilt that protected Rosalia from the cold was a collection of matching sixteen-inch by sixteen-inch squares sewn together. Each square contained a repeating symmetrical hexagon design of orange cloth stitched onto the white squares. The quilt was given to Rosalia by her mother as a wedding gift and was showing wear from over ten years of use. Rosalia wore a faded long flannel nightshirt that was colored soft pink, a present from Gottlieb two Christmases earlier. She loved the feel of this nightshirt and wore it often in the winter months.

Rosalia's maiden name was Kramer. She was born in America to immigrant parents and grew up in a German household in the country outside of Fowler. She had a slight frame, with lustrous shoulder-length brown hair. Before her illness, Rosalia was full of energy. She possessed an outgoing personality and took time to be kind and thoughtful to all. Her mannerisms earned her the respect and love of all who knew her. She was athletic, being among the fastest runners in her class when she graduated eighth grade, her final year of schooling in Fowler. When she attended the singles dances at the Sturgis Opera House in Fowler, she would rarely stop dancing until the musicians finally quit for the evening. Many an eyebrow was raised when she began to spend time with Gottlieb. It seemed that they were complete opposites, which is perhaps what attracted them to each other.

She married Gottlieb at the age of 24, welcoming their first son Francis into the world just ten months after they wed. Rosalia loved the farm life. She especially enjoyed collecting eggs, picking wild raspberries, growing her garden, canning produce, and the chores of maintaining a proper farm home. Rosalia was a very good cook, but her health had diminished significantly during this winter season, and she no longer had the energy for the simplest of tasks. When Francis and Clem entered the room, she managed a smile and raised her right outstretched hand as a signal for them to come and sit by her. Her boys joined her, sitting one at each side of her bed while Gottlieb stood quietly in the doorway. She coughed slightly, with barely the strength to make a sound.

Rosalia turned her head toward Francis on her right and placed her hand on his arm. She managed a smile and said with labored breath, "I'm going to leave soon. I want you to know how much I love you. Grow up strong, always be polite, and take care of Clem."

Then she turned to Clem. In her left hand was a handkerchief stained with blood from persistent, earlier coughing. She did not move to touch him. She said, "Clem, my baby, I've been wanting to tell you something ..."

She began to cough, slightly at first, and then more intensely. Rosalia brought her handkerchief to her mouth, and for ten agonizing seconds she coughed until it seemed all of the remaining strength within her thirty-five-year-old body was gone. Her chest grew still, and she took on a look of death. Clem threw his arms around her and began to sob. Francis started crying as well. Gottlieb stood motionless in the doorway. He agonized deep inside about how his life had taken another wicked turn. Clem would never learn what it was that his mother wanted to tell him.

"Rosalia lies there next to Clem," Margot said, pointing to a small gravestone.

I turned to see a simple moss-covered grave marker, which read: Rosalia Sohn, 1884–1919.

Margot continued ...

Francis and Clem were affected deeply by the death of their mother. Clem cried for days. Gottlieb actually stopped drinking for a short while and was very responsible taking care of the necessary arrangements for Rosalia. Her body lay in state in their home for three days while friends and family came to visit and express their condolences.

The memorial service for Rosalia took place on March 4, 1919. It was one of the coldest days of the winter season, with blistering winds. It was a very long day, beginning with Rosalia's body being taken from their home and brought to the Catholic Church in

Fowler. This vision of Rosalia's casket being closed and taken from their home finally made her death real for Clem. Up to that point, he had felt that maybe this was simply a big mistake, that at any time she would sit up and speak with him again. A church service was performed, then a potluck gathering of family and well-wishers was held at the village hall in Fowler. By the time Molly brought Gottlieb and the boys home that evening in their open buckboard, the fire had gone completely out in the wood stove that heated their home. Clem shivered profusely until a new fire was started and the kitchen in the old farmhouse warmed up again.

Within a month, Gottlieb had reached a new low point in his life. There were signs of spring in the air, which meant the beginning of tilling and planting. Gottlieb was no longer interested in farming, and he detested living in the home that had at one time meant everything to Rosalia and him. His drinking intensified, and he stopped maintaining the house and farm. Francis and Clem did everything they could to keep the animals fed and watered, but as the root cellar supplies dwindled and the store of hay and grain diminished, they grew weary of their situation as well.

Fortunately, Rosalia's sisters came to the rescue. Francis moved to stay with Rosalia's sister Maggie, who had married a Motz and lived several miles east of their homestead, while Clem moved in with Rosalia's sister Catherine (called Deanie), who had married a Kissane and lived about four and a half miles farther south and east of the Motz farm. Both of these farms were in neighboring St. Johns.

Gottlieb heard of openings in the Lansing Police Department, about thirty miles southeast of Fowler, from his brother Charles. Charles was on the police force at the time and was able to put in a good word for Gottlieb, who then gained employment. Gottlieb left the farm to start a new life. After hiring on with the police force, Gottlieb settled into a home on the east side of Lansing, while his sons continued to live on separate farms in the St. Johns area. For the next six years, Gottlieb would see his sons only a couple of times each year.

Margot appeared somewhat gloomy to me. I could tell she had difficulty talking about Clem's childhood.

"Did Clem and Francis ever get to see each other?" I asked.

Margot replied, "Although Francis and Clem lived about five miles apart, they saw each other often. They both attended schools in the St. Johns area and developed a love for American baseball."

BATTER UP!

"**B**aseball?" I asked.

"Oh yes," Margot responded, "baseball! In fact, Francis gained a nickname through baseball. Clem told me his brother was a terrific pitcher, and Clem was his catcher."

Margot continued her recollection of these young brothers' lives and how baseball helped to keep them in touch with each other as they grew older.

With the death of Rosalia and their move away from the Sohn farmhouse, both Francis and Clem became very independent. The transitions into their new homes worked out well for both. They were each polite and helpful in their new environments, but they had wide latitude to make their own decisions about how they spent their free time. Both the Motz and Kissane families were sensitive to the need for these brothers to see each other regularly. Often, when one farm family was going in the direction of the other, they brought their Sohn guest along to drop them off or pick up the other. The siblings were loved and treasured by both households.

There was one thing the Sohn brothers prized, and that was playing catch. When they spent time together in the summer, they would often fill each other in on the latest news while pitching a baseball back and forth. With a focus on accuracy, they often played a game where the ball of the thrower must be catchable by the other without moving the position of the catcher's feet. They would move around the yard, stop to plant, and wait to catch the other's throw. This game developed good muscle memory for both to throw very accurately.

Francis threw with his left hand and developed a good command of his pitches. He listened to the Detroit Tigers on the radio and dreamed of becoming a great pitcher like Hooks Dauss. He had obtained a Pitcher's Guidebook from the five-and-dime store for two pennies and began to experiment with different ways of holding a baseball while throwing. Both Francis and Clem were able to purchase Zenith-brand webbed baseball gloves from Gower's Hardware Store in St. Johns using allowance money they earned working on their respective farms.

When Clem and Francis played catch, they would sometimes act out a major league game, with Francis winning it in the last inning with the final pitch of the game.

"It's the bottom of the ninth folks, and Francis Sohn is on the mound," Clem announced, lowering his voice and imitating the professional tones he had picked up from Ty Tyson on the Detroit Tigers radio broadcasts. "The bases are loaded, and the Sultan of Swat, the Babe … that's right folks, *Babe Ruth* is at the plate. The Detroit Tigers are up by one run, and the bases are loaded. There are two strikes on the Yankees slugger, and this is a do-or-die pitch for Francis Sohn."

Clem threw the ball he'd recently caught back to Francis for this last game-winning pitch, continuing his dialogue.

"The Great Bambino steps out of the batter's box and points his bat at the right-field fence. Could this be a home run coming up? Catcher Clem Sohn gives Francis the sign for an extreme change-up by pressing the palm of his hand downward. Francis likes the sign, nods his head, and then stares at the Bronx Bomber. Suddenly, a smile spreads across Francis' face, and the Babe looks confused. The amazing pitcher goes into his windup and lets the ball go. His arm speed is tremendous, yet the pitch quickly loses speed. The Bambino swings with all his might but is way ahead of the ball, which hits the ground in front of the plate. The Tigers win the ball game and the World Series by a score of four to three, and the crowd goes wild!!"

When an opportunity presented itself for the boys to join a baseball league in St. Johns, both caretaker families met it with approval.

"What nickname did Francis earn on the baseball team?" I asked.

"Oh, I almost forgot about that," Margot chuckled. "I didn't mean to be a twit … it was *Lefty*.

"Several years after Rosalia died, Lefty and Clem joined a baseball team that played in St. Johns. Lefty played in the infield and also pitched, while Clem was the team catcher.

"Clem told me about a fantastic game they played to win a league tournament championship. Lefty and Clem pulled a silly trick on a batter to win the game," Margot said with a smile.

On a warm Saturday in August, the Pohl Brothers and Steel Hotel teams met to settle the championship of their league. The game was played on a baseball field near the St. Johns high school. It had a large backstop and green wooden dugouts on each side. The field itself was rough and uneven, but the grass was mowed, and the base paths were well-marked from continual use throughout the summer. There was no pitcher's mound, just a wooden board anchored to the dirt with two long, metal pegs. Home plate was a flat diamond-shaped board also anchored to the dirt, and the bases were burlap bags filled with straw. They were not fastened to the ground, but well-worn spots in the field indicated their proper locations. This was a beautiful day for baseball, with a slight breeze from the southwest that helped push the ball toward the right-field fence. Majestic white clouds sailed across the sky, providing occasional temporary relief from the sun.

The Sohn siblings played on the Pohl Brothers Chevrolet team, and on this day, they were up for the challenge against the Steel Hotel team. The league was comprised of five teams, and each team played all the others twice to make up the season. This was a winner-take-all championship game, as both the Pohl Brothers and Steel Hotel teams ended up with a 7-1 record. The only games these two teams had lost were to the other. On this particular day, both teams had played very well in the early innings. They were now at the bottom of the seventh and last inning of the game. The Pohl Brothers team was ahead three to two. There were two outs on the Steel Hotel team, but the bases were loaded with their best batter stepping up to the plate.

The Pohl Brothers team sported aged woolen uniforms, which were white in color with a blue bow-tie Chevrolet logo cut out of felt and stitched onto the front of each shirt. White six-panel ball caps with a blue bill and a blue button on the top were also part of the outfit. A large, red number was cut from felt and hand-stitched on the back of each shirt.

The Steel Hotel team had much newer uniforms, in only their second year of use. These uniforms were light gray in color and sported the words STEEL HOTEL on the front of the jersey. Their caps were gray to match the uniforms, with a black bill and button on the top. The uniforms also had large numbers stitched to the back made of black felt.

Tank Thelen was the next player to step up to the plate for the Steel Hotel team. He was big for his age. He stood 5 feet 11 inches. He grew up on a farm south of St. Johns and was country-strong, like the Sohn brothers. Tank was a bit of a bully. He was going into the eighth grade and was used to getting his way. He had tangled with Lefty just a few weeks earlier over a silly matter, which boys have the occasion to do. Tank had offered Lefty either a knuckle sandwich or walk-away. When Lefty stood his ground, Tank eventually backed down, but he'd nursed a lingering grudge ever since their confrontation. Tank had already reached base safely each of the three times he batted earlier in the game.

Lefty was playing shortstop on this particular day. Herm Pohl, the coach of the Pohl Brothers team, could see that his pitcher, Wilbur "Brownie" Brown, was spent, so he called time out. As he walked to the pitcher's mound, he motioned for Lefty to finish pitching the game.

Herm joined Clem, Brownie, and Lefty on the mound and said, "Lefty, throw a few wild pitches during warm-up and get this kid thinking you're no good. Then fan him! Brownie, you take over at short."

Lefty nodded, and Herm walked off the field. Tank grinned and yelled out to Lefty as he exited the Steel Hotel dugout.

"Hey, doofus, do you think you can get me out? Well think again doofus!" He started laughing loudly.

Lefty was now determined to make Tank look like a fool.

Sitting in the stands on the first-base side was the prettiest girl in Lefty's class by the name of Rita Fields. Rita was thin and delicate-seeming, with beautiful blue eyes. She had soft blonde hair and was beginning to show signs of becoming a woman, which did not go unnoticed by the boys in school. Lefty had a crush on her, as did most all of the boys. He looked over at her before his first warm-up pitch. She noticed and cast a smile in his direction.

Tank had feelings for Rita as well. He would try to sit near her during lunch at school, which meant she was off limits to all the other boys who were lower in the pecking order. Lefty wanted to make a chump out of Tank in the worst way, and it would be all the better if he could do it in front of Rita. This had become more than a game to both of these players … it was personal! Tank had grabbed his favorite Spalding wooden bat and walked to the batter's on-deck area to take a few swings as Lefty prepared to face him.

Lefty gripped the ball and threw the first warm-up pitch way above Clem. Clem jumped up to catch it, but it flew a few feet above his outstretched hand and hit the backstop behind him.

"Hey, doofus, are you trying to throw over the backstop? You can't even do that, can you?" Tank yelled out. He began to laugh again as he turned toward Rita, acting like a bantam cockerel fluffing his feathers.

Lefty gripped the ball and threw his second warm-up pitch into the dirt about three feet in front of the plate. It bounced into Clem's waiting glove.

"Hey, doofus, I think you just killed a gopher with that pitch!" Tank shouted with great volume. By now the people in the bleachers were beginning to enjoy the banter and laughed at Tank's insulting verbal jabs. This reaction from the crowd encouraged Tank all the more.

However, Lefty was unfazed by Tank's abuse. He gripped the ball and threw his last warm-up pitch far right of the plate, beyond Clem's reach. Clem could not catch this ball, and it struck the backstop like Lefty's first pitch, almost hitting the unsuspecting umpire.

"Hey, doofus, that's one way to win the game … kill the ump!" Tank bellowed in response to Lefty's errant pitch. This time the laughter of the crowd was very loud and long. Tank puffed up his chest, clearly full of himself and his clever verbal abuse.

"Batter up!" cried the ump, who was a little shaken from the near-miss pitch. He looked at Tank with disdain for his comment.

As Tank stepped up to the plate, he took an unusually long amount of time getting set. He was enjoying this immensely. In his mind, he thought the best way to make Lefty look like a fool was to simply take a walk to tie the game. Tank had seen Lefty pitch in his last league game a few days earlier; in the latter innings, he'd had control issues that nearly lost the game for his team. As bad as Lefty had warmed up today, he thought he could take four balls, and the next batter up would be able to do the same. Tank's plan was to let the first pitch go by, so he stood with the bat resting limply on his shoulder.

Clem gave the sign for a curveball. Lefty nodded, wound up for the pitch, and threw a perfect curveball right into the middle of the strike zone.

"Steerrriike!" yelled the umpire.

Tank backed out of the batter's box to collect himself. This was totally unexpected of Lefty, and there was an immediate buzz of excitement in the crowd. They again grew silent as Tank stepped forward into the box and stood for the next pitch.

Clem gave the sign for a fastball. At this point, Tank was still thinking that Lefty had made a lucky pitch and decided to appear prepared to swing, but to let this next pitch go by as well. He was sure it would be an errant throw and desperately wanted Lefty to lose the game for the Pohl Brothers team.

Lefty went through his delivery and threw another perfect pitch down the middle of the strike zone. This pitch had a lot of speed to it, blowing by a somewhat shocked Tank.

"Steerrriike twooo!" the umpire roared after the second pitch.

The crowd grew louder, as this was an unexpected chain of events. Tank stepped out of the batter's box again; this time, he really began to worry about what was going to happen next. Beads of sweat rolled down from Tank's forehead as he swung his bat a couple of times to try and refocus. He stepped back into the batter's box. His attitude had changed completely now, as he wanted nothing more than to belt the ball as hard as he could.

"I'm gonna kill this pitch," Tank whispered to himself, sweat dripping steadily from the broad tip of his nose.

"Hey, Tank, do you inhale or exhale when you swing?" asked Clem before issuing the next sign.

Tank didn't answer, instead backing quickly out of the batter's box. He suddenly wondered how he handled his breath when he swung. He drew a quick inhalation, then let a quick breath out as he swung his bat. He looked back with contempt at Clem, who was smiling broadly at him. Tank shook his head and turned toward Lefty.

Clem remembered the baseball fantasy that Lefty and he played out so often when they tossed the ball around. Clem spread his fingers and palm open as if to push on the ground like he used to do. This was not a normal pitching sign and was not taught or used by the team. Lefty had not seen Clem give this sign for over a year in their backyard, but he recognized it immediately and knew what to do. Lefty could not help but smile broadly when he gave Clem the nod for acceptance of the sign.

Herm, their coach, viewed the unusual sign Clem gave to Lefty and said quietly, "What the hell?"

Tank looked into Lefty's eyes with grim determination, incredibly anxious to rip the cowhide off of the baseball with his ferocious swing. When he saw Lefty smiling, he gritted his teeth and gripped the bat tightly. Lefty looked at the crowd and gave a small, quick nod to Rita, then pulled his body back for the pitch. His arm came forward quickly but then abruptly slowed, the baseball leaving his hand at a low, sluggish trajectory. Tank misjudged the force of the pitch in his fury to hit the ball and swung well ahead of it. The ball hit the ground a few feet in front of the plate and rolled into Clem's waiting catcher's mitt.

"Steerrriike threeee!" the umpire called.

The Pohl Brothers team had won the game.

As the jubilant victors ran to their coach to prepare for the team handshake, Tank walked slowly to the Steel Hotel dugout dragging his bat. He was again outwitted by Lefty and felt he had lost the game.

This would not be the last time Clem had dealings with Tank.

"That story is funny," I said, jotting down a few notes. "I'm glad they won the game. It sounds like Clem and Francis were quite a devilish duo. I was the catcher on my high school softball team, so I can really relate. Did you play ball when you were young?"

"Me?" Margot responded.

"Yes ... what was your childhood like? Did you grow up on a farm in England?" I asked, eager to learn all about this new friend of mine.

RICKSHAW RIDE

"I didn't play baseball," Margot responded. "I was involved in something quite different. Instead of baseball cleats, I spent my time in baffies. I was a ballerina, and if I must say so myself, I was rather good!" She winked.

"What are baffies?" I asked.

Margot giggled and explained, "Baffies are what I called the ballet slippers I danced in. I still remember the first time I set foot in a dance studio—it changed my life forever.

"I wasn't called Margot at that time; that's my stage name. When I was a little girl, I was known as Margaret ... Margaret Hookham."

"Come here, Margaret, we mustn't be late!" cried Mrs. Hilda Hookham to her four-year-old daughter. Hilda was a determined lady. She had thick, dark hair and an athletic build for her four-feet eleven-inch frame. She had always wanted to dance, but her life's path had not allowed for it; she was not about to let her own daughter miss the opportunity she had failed to seize. On this important day, she had donned a heavy coat and pulled rubber boots over her shoes to keep out the mist and cold.

Little Margaret was in her bedroom dressed in a cream-colored pullover dress, which was knee-high in length. She was all set to go to her first dance lesson. Before her mom's call, Margaret took some time to pretend to dance in a contemporary fashion she had recently seen at a wedding reception. She danced energetically around her bed and jumped a time or two on her bed as well. She loved the wild movements of the modern dances she had seen. Margaret knew that today she would be attending her first dance lesson and could not wait to arrive at the studio.

Margaret's house was located on 44 Waldeck Road in London, England. It was a typical residential home with three small bedrooms, a kitchen, a dining area, a small bathroom with a chain-pull flush toilet, and a sitting room for family gatherings. The house featured dark, hardwood floors that announced movement throughout the dwelling with indiscriminate creaking sounds. The rooms had large, single-paned windows, which allowed natural sunlight to pour into the home. This residence was small but rather cozy for Margaret, her brother Felix Edward, and her parents.

Upon hearing her mother's call, Margaret exited her bedroom and ran to the front door to thrust her arms into the waiting coat her mother was holding. She then put on her boots and mittens before taking her mom's hand and heading out the door. With anxious expectation, she walked down the porch steps to the street and turned right for the four-block excursion to the Bosustow School of Dance. On this September day, the temperature was cool, the chilly promise of fall hovering in the damp air.

When she arrived at the studio, Margaret passed through a garden gate, then climbed a short flight of concrete steps and entered through a thick-paneled door with her mom. When the door opened, Margaret immediately heard the unfamiliar sound of dance shoes softly sliding and landing on a studio floor to the beat of music from Tchaikovsky's *Iolanta* opera, played by a pianist. She followed her mom down a short hallway, the doorway to a dance floor coming into view. She looked into the room from whence the noise emanated and saw seven young ballerinas. They were dancing in two lines facing a wall, which was covered lengthwise with seven-foot-tall mirrors. Three feet above the floor in front of the mirrors was a railing, which was supported by brass brackets every four feet for the full length of the wall. An adjoining wall had a wonderful full-length fireplace devouring split oak wood, taking the chill out of the dance studio. The floor was covered with linoleum, which was deep green in color. On the wall opposite the mirrors hung a somewhat large picture of Dame Adeline Genée showing the five positions of arms in ballet. This was strategically placed so that the young ballerinas could see it in the background as they critiqued themselves in the mirror.

The ballerinas were dancing in graceful harmony—at least, it looked harmonious to young Margaret. The skilled eyes of Grace Bosustow, the dance instructor, revealed quite a different picture. After a minute or so of dance, Grace could take it no longer.

"Mrs. Langford, can you please stop playing," Grace requested of the pianist in an elevated tone.

"Girls, girls," Grace said as she turned to the ballerinas, "you must not only know the steps, but you must feel the music. Do not simply transfer from one movement to another, but flow to them. Think of what you would want to see in a dancer, and perform it for yourself and your audience.

"Move your arms and hands with elegance and determination. Now, please take a few minutes to practice among yourselves," Grace suggested.

Grace then made her way to Margaret and Hilda, who were awaiting a formal introduction.

"Hello, Mrs. Hookham," greeted Grace. "It is so nice to see you again."

"Please call me Hilda," Mrs. Hookham responded.

"I will, and you may call me Grace," Miss Bosustow responded in kind. "I am very pleased that you decided to have your daughter learn ballet here."

"The other studios I visited did not make me feel as welcome as this one has," Hilda responded. "I am anxious for Margaret to get started."

"Well, I am chuffed to bits to have her here," Grace excitedly replied.

Grace turned to Margaret and asked, "Margaret, are you ready to join the rest of the dance troupe?"

Margaret was intently watching the ballerinas work with each other, becoming so engrossed she didn't even hear the conversation her mom and Miss Bosustow were having. She had never seen anyone wear a tutu before, and the funny-looking footwear with unusually long toes looked strange and most uncomfortable. The occasional rise to the dancer's tip-toes not only looked painful, but was not at all what she was expecting. She did not think she wanted to learn this rather sedate form of dance. It was not the wild tapping she had practiced in her bedroom less than an hour earlier.

"Margaret," Hilda called in a loud voice, "please answer Miss Bosustow's question!"

Margaret turned and said, "Yes," without knowing exactly what she was agreeing to.

"Very well," Grace said, "I think I have the proper shoes and dress for you to wear. Please follow me."

Grace turned to Hilda and said, "You may leave if you'd like and come back in an hour or so."

"I do have some errands to run. I'll be back in an hour," Hilda responded to Grace.

"Now listen closely to Miss Bosustow," Hilda instructed Margaret as she turned and made her way to the door.

"I felt a wee bit abandoned by Mum that day," Margot confessed to me. "But after a few months of training, I began to focus and appreciate the beauty of the ballet.

"The tutu and baffies seemed dreadful to me at first, but after a time I saw their usefulness. To tell the truth, they became rather dishy to me," Margot said with a twinkle in her eye. "I quickly took to ballet and discovered that it gave me confidence as a small child. My mum came to the studio often and did much of the sewing required to keep our dance costumes looking tidy and presentable.

"Just two years later, when I was six, Mum took me to see Anna Pavlova, the famous Russian ballerina. At that time, Anna was ballyhooed as the best ballerina in the world. What a marvelous performance she gave!" Margot gushed. "She was so light on her feet that she seemed to fly across the stage, as if suspended from above.

"I probably had a bit of a chip on my shoulder at that young age. Because of my desire to excel, I had become one of the best young dancers at Miss Bosustow's dance studio. When I saw Anna perform, two thoughts struck me: she was indeed a wonderful dancer, and I would someday dance just as well as she.

"I suppose that sense of flying through the air in ballet was part of an exhilaration shared by Clem and me," Margot mused. Then, becoming somewhat sullen, she continued:

"In November of 1927, my world would change completely."

The winter weather was menacing on this cold November morning. Soft, blowing snow was piling up on the outside windowsills as the streets and sidewalks slowly surrendered their dull-gray coloring to a layer of bright, new snow. The head of the household, Felix

John Hookham, had already carefully built a warm fire in the main stove located in the sitting room. He called his son Felix Edward and daughter Margaret to assemble with his wife Hilda and himself for a family discussion. When Margaret entered, she saw her father decked out in a gray suit with a white shirt and a light-purple ascot tie with a paisley pattern, which was unusual for a Saturday morning. By the outside doorway sat a small suitcase and a clothes bag, which Margaret noted had been used in the past for packing clothes to go on summer holiday. Hilda was standing by John, showing support for what was about to be said.

"I have something very important to tell you children," Felix began softly, the sound of the crackling fireplace competing with his words. "I have accepted a position with the British American Tobacco Company in Shanghai, China. This position has come to my attention rather suddenly, and I am leaving for Shanghai within the hour."

World War I had ended just nine years earlier. Over nine million soldiers had lost their lives in the bloody trenches all across Europe. Millions more would come back home addicted to the nicotine found in the cigarettes, which were made readily available to the troops. Tobacco products were in high demand at this time. The position Felix had accepted was as a chief engineer, and the salary for his services was much too great for him to turn down.

At her tender age, Margaret couldn't fully grasp what this meant. Her initial reaction was unemotional: She didn't understand the distance to be traveled and the cultural changes she would someday experience.

"I will be traveling for the next few weeks before arriving in Shanghai, China, and will look for a new house for us all as soon as I am able," Felix said with pride-filled confidence. "It won't be long and we'll all be together again on this wonderful adventure."

"I didn't see my father for over half a year after that day," Margot said rather forlornly. "When I was just a tyke, Daddy tried to spend a great deal of individual time with me whenever he could. I was always his special little girl, and it was very difficult not seeing his face each day. I continued to dance; to be honest, it was dance that helped get me through the loneliness I felt. It kept me from having too much free time to think and made me tired so that I could drift off to sleep each night. But I did miss my father ever so much.

"By this time, I was nine years old, and I noticed something even at that young age. Many of the girls taking instruction at the dance studio did not really have their hearts in it. They were there because their mums wanted them to dance, I suppose," Margot intimated.

"But wasn't that true of your mom as well?" I asked.

"Yes, that's true," answered Margot, "but it had quite a different meaning for me once I experienced it for myself. The other girls just didn't take to dance in the manner that I did."

I wasn't sure I understood completely what she meant, but I didn't want to belabor the issue. I wanted to hear more about her life. So far, I'd already filled up three pages of notebook paper.

"In May of 1928, my father came home on leave. When his time to return to Shanghai came due, Mum and I left England to go live with my father," Margot continued. "Brother Felix was eleven years old and did not travel with us to Shanghai. Instead, he stayed back with my grandparents in Devon. We would never live together as a family again.

"There was a Sino-Japanese conflict at that time, which made it too dangerous to travel from England to China via an eastern route. My parents and I traveled across the Atlantic to the United States to avoid this military struggle. We landed in New York and then spent the next month traveling by train across the United States."

"That must have been a wonderful adventure," I exclaimed.

Margot replied, "It was actually somewhat frightening at first. We didn't know what we would encounter at each stop. The scenery was beautiful in some parts of this country but was also very flat and uninteresting in others. With all of the dancing I had been doing, it was very difficult to suddenly spend so much of my time sitting. At every stop, I would stretch, jump, and dance to the amusement of the other passengers. We finally arrived in Seattle, Washington, and boarded the SS President Jackson to set sail for China. The ship ride across the Pacific Ocean was uneventful, and I longed to be back on land. I still remember stepping off the ship in Shanghai. I had never been in such a busy port city in my life. So many ships, so many people, and so much smoke pouring from factory buildings that it darkened the sky. My father was well adapted to the culture. He flagged a rickshaw down to carry our luggage and us to our home several blocks away."

"I've seen rickshaws in pictures. They seem like an odd means of transport," I noted.

"Yes. A strange two-wheeled cart, which was used as sort of a taxi in that bustling city. There is a seat between two very large wheels, and the cart has two long poles extending out in front. A man steps between the poles, grabs one in each hand, picks them up, and pulls the cart to the requested destination." Margot spoke with arm gestures to emphasize her point.

"It was a dreadful experience at first, having a person act as a horse," she continued. "I had difficulty getting used to the slight bobbing I felt with each running step. But it turned out to be a fairly efficient means of getting around the city. I was rather used to it by the time we left Shanghai years later."

"What about your dance training?" I asked, feeling a little concerned about this pastime that had become so important to her.

"If you knew my mum, you would know she would never let me give up dance," Margot replied.

"By this time people in the dance community had started to

notice me. Mum looked for the best school for dance that she could find; my father was rather well-to-do with his position in the tobacco company, and money was no longer the scarce commodity it had been back home in England.

"There was a marvelous Russian instructor in Shanghai by the name of George Goncharov. Mum found him based on recommendations from the Society of Ladies, which she quickly became a part of," Margot explained. "George worked diligently with me and continued to advance my dancing skills, pushing me beyond what I had learned back in England.

"I went to school at the Cathedral School for Girls, which was run by a head mistress named Miss Fleet. She was a loud, determined lady who terrorized students and parents alike. I did not at all appreciate the schooling I received there until much later in life. Miss Fleet demanded structure and consistency. With all that I accomplished in the future, this regimented lifestyle would prove to be exactly what I needed. I did not gad about like many of the girls did back then."

"How long did you stay in Shanghai?" I asked.

"I was there nearly six years," Margot responded. "Mum was constantly being reminded by everyone how much I had progressed in ballet. She worried that I would not get a chance to showcase my dance talents to the world if I stayed in Shanghai much longer.

"Shanghai had also put a tremendous strain on my parents," Margot continued. "Mum discovered quickly that she didn't really like being away from England. Father's job was quite demanding. He worked long hours, and sometimes wouldn't come home for days. Though they largely kept their feelings from me, I could tell that they were not at all happy with the arrangement. Father became more and more distant toward us. When Mum decided to move back to England, it seemed to be a great relief for both of them," Margot recalled, a forsaken look in her eyes.

"Mum made plans, and we took a ship back to London when

I was fourteen years old. To her, it was a pivotal moment in my career. She wanted me back in England where I could be evaluated against some of the best ballet talent at that time," Margot explained.

"This was 1934, and a very strange time in history indeed. Adolf Hitler was gaining power in Germany and became Führer in the late summer. Of course, we didn't know at the time, but this was a prelude to World War II. I came back home, and Mum immediately took me to the Sadler Wells Theatre for a talent assessment by the Vic Wells Ballet troupe. Because of the schooling I had received in Shanghai, I had advanced significantly beyond the rest of the dancers I had left in England.

"Ninette de Valois did the assessment, and afterward she immediately put me in touch with Fredrick Ashton. Fredrick was a skilled dancer and choreographer. He created wonderful dance presentations like *Swan Lake, Ondine, Daphnis and Chloe,* and *Sylvia,* which were among his finest works," Margot recalled.

"I was placed under his tutelage, but I must admit I did not like Frederick one smidgen at first. He was loud and rough and did not seem to recognize my talent. He swore at me continually and grabbed me with big strong hands to move me into proper position. He smelled of perspiration and cigar and was dreadful to work with. At first, I fought him and continued to dance in the ways I had been taught up to that point. I was quite stubborn and content with my abilities. I cried in my bedroom many nights, wondering if I should continue," Margot admitted with a sigh.

"Then one evening I had had enough. In the middle of one of his rants, I stopped, fell to the floor, and burst into tears. I told him between sobs, 'I don't want to fight with you anymore. I will do what you are asking me to do.' I didn't realize it at the time, but this is what Fredrick needed from me. I was never going to improve doing things in the manner I had learned up to that time. I needed to take my talents to another level."

Margot's statement cut to my own heart. I had also been content with my writing ability. Perhaps I needed to stretch in new ways to become something greater than I was at that time, or any time before. Maybe this story was what I needed to positively change my own life. I scribbled furiously.

Margot continued, "After I submitted to his training, my dance practices rose to new heights. Fredrick challenged me to pay attention to every little movement of my entire body. I even carefully planned the movements of the tips of my fingers to create a complete expression of the music. Soon, my ballet was bringing audiences to tears. I will never forget how that awful monster of a choreographer became my greatest influence. He taught a hoofer like me to become one of the premier dancers of my day."

"That must have been difficult," I conjectured.

"More than you will ever know," Margot replied. "But, I will forever be in debt to Fredrick for not giving up on me while I rebelled against him.

"As I continued to work with Fredrick, my reputation spread. I was asked to perform as the featured dancer in amazing and wonderful numbers," she continued. "The Vic Wells Ballet would later become the Britain Royal Ballet, and I was the featured dancer in the troupe. It was then that I changed my name from Margaret Hookham to Margot Fonteyn."

"Why Fonteyn?" I wondered out loud.

"It comes from the word 'font,' which means fountain. There was a little fountain I found in a small park in Shanghai. It was always so peaceful, yet lively. The water always flowed, and the pool never emptied. It seemed to sooth me during the dark times in Shanghai. I suppose you could say my last name came from Shanghai, though I would not bring anything else back from that foreign place," Margot explained.

"Did you have a chance to see your brother again?"

"Oh yes. Little Felix and I quickly grew close after I came back to London. He cared so much for me and helped me in so many ways. He is still my closest friend in the whole world."

"And your father …" I inquired.

"Father was imprisoned in Shanghai by the Japanese for two and a half years after the war broke out. When he finally did come home in 1945, he brought with him a new wife … named Beatrice. She was a rather ghastly woman who did not like Mum or me in the least," Margot explained. "Father had become a very different person, and I could no longer relate to him. He did attend some of my performances, but his pride was too great to ever tell me what he thought. I did not even know when he died in 1976 until almost a year later. It is rather amazing to see where life has taken you when you look back over time … don't you think?"

OL' PUDDINS

"You sure have lived an interesting life!" I exclaimed.

"I guess I did at that," replied Margot. "But while I was traversing about the world dancing ballet, Clem was beginning to make a name for himself as an aviator.

"Clem lived with his adopted family, the Kissanes, until his father remarried. Gottlieb married a woman name Louise about five years after he moved to Lansing. Louise was very different from Clem's Mum Rosalia. Where Rosalia was spirited and somewhat adventurous, Louise was rather withdrawn and timid. Gottlieb took on an increasingly controlling character, which Louise reluctantly accepted. Gottlieb was 44 years of age when he married Louise, and she was only 32. Clem did not relate well to Louise," Margot said.

"In September 1926, after Gottlieb's wedding, Clem moved to Lansing to live with his parents. Clem was very independent, had few inhibitions, was a bit of a clown, and quickly made friends in his new surroundings," Margot noted. "He went to the new Eastern High School in Lansing and was a part of its second graduating class. This was a considerable change from the school he left in St. Johns. Clem was involved in the Aviation Club and the Knights of

Industry in high school. Clem told me that next to his yearbook picture, it reads: *A steady man is he ...*" Margot chuckled a little after recalling this. "He was a steady man for sure. There was one thing Clem really loved to do whenever he could ..."

"Let me guess," I interrupted, "fly in an airplane?"

"You are quite right, young lass. Clem loved to be in a plane cockpit," Margot replied.

She began to articulate how it was that Clem began flying with his friend Art Davis.

Art Davis was cruising at an altitude of 5,600 feet over Davis Airport, an airfield located about two miles north of East Lansing Michigan on Chandler Road. He was flying his WACO Taperwing airplane on this unusually clear and warm June 12 in 1927. Art's airplane was painted bright yellow with big black letters on each side reading, *AirDevil Airplane Company.*

Art was an Army Major in World War I. He received flight training in the army, and it was always a part of his life thereafter. After leaving military service, he became a stunt flyer and racer who loved to dip and turn his plane to test the limits of its maneuverability. On this Sunday afternoon, he was executing a series of loops and rolls in preparation for an upcoming air show in Battle Creek.

As he flew, Art looked down and noticed a gentleman standing next to a bicycle at the far south hangar, intently watching him fly. He had seen this unknown visitor before. On this particular day, Art swooped down toward the interested guest and gave a salute as he sailed by. Art's wave was met in kind by Clem's. Clem was completely captivated by this exhibition of flight.

After taxiing to the airport office, Art noticed that Clem was still standing by the hangar watching another pilot prepare for a takeoff. Unaware of who Clem was, Art entered his 1926 Oldsmobile DR Tourer near the airport office and drove one-quarter mile to the south hangar to find out more about this stranger. Clem was tall for his age. At nearly five feet eleven inches, Art thought he was riding up to an older gentleman.

"I've seen you here before, haven't I?" asked Art after stepping out of his automobile and moving toward Clem.

"Yes," replied a confident Clem, "I come here occasionally to watch the flying machines take off and land. Flying must be the most wonderful thing a man can do."

Art looked Clem up and down. Clem appeared to be strong and energetic. He seemed to have the same unusual passion for flight that he himself had. This was appealing to Art.

"My name is Art Davis, and I operate Michigan Airways. I could use some part-time help around here. How old are you?" Art asked, holding out his oil-stained hand.

"I'm sixteen, and I can start right now if you'd like," Clem responded, giving Art a firm handshake in return.

"I think you should go back home and ask your parents first," Art directed.

"I have been living without my parents for the better part of five years," Clem responded. "They don't really care what I do."

Art was surprised at this response.

"Okay. I'll take you on, son, but if your parents complain even once, you will have to leave," Art retorted.

"Clem was already living a life very independent of his parents. He worked several weeks at Michigan Airways before Gottlieb and Louise even knew he was employed there. Clem was making a good wage of twelve cents per hour sweeping the hangars, repairing equipment, and mowing the turf airstrips," Margot explained.

"Every so often, when the work was caught up, Art would take Clem up in one of his airplanes. Clem loved to ride with Art as he flew over the Michigan countryside. Art grew very fond of Clem, and it wasn't long before he taught Clem how to fly his plane."

Margot paused and wiped at her eyes, smiling nostalgically. "Art was paid by individual pilots to maintain the airport and store their airplanes," she said after a moment. "Flying at that time was unique. An airplane in the skies would cause people to pause what they were doing and take a look up.

"As a stunt pilot, Art would perform at air shows, twisting and turning in his plane in ways not normally seen by the average person. Air shows were a big sensation in those days, drawing tens of thousands of spectators each weekend. Everyone loved watching stunt flying and the pilots. The risks they took excited the crowds. Clem wanted desperately to be a stunt flyer, but Art would not let him. 'Stick to your schoolbooks,' Art would say. 'Your time for flying will come.' However, by the time Clem graduated from Eastern High School in 1929, he was a veteran pilot. He had flown hundreds of hours in several different airplanes. One of the things Clem was known for was buzzing people with his plane."

"Buzzing?" I asked, needing more clarification for my notes.

"I had to ask Clem about this term myself," Margot recalled. "It is when you fly a plane toward an unsuspecting mate on the ground to scare them. The view of a plane heading right at you is a very scary sight, I was told."

Margot chuckled and began to tell of a specific time Clem buzzed someone.

Bill Kissane, Clem's adopted father, was working on the roof of his chicken hutch. At sixty-six years of age, Bill was a wiry farmer used to hard work and well able to handle this task. The old wooden shingles on the coop were beginning to wear with age and needed to be selectively replaced. This summer day in 1928 was a hot one, and Bill was continually wiping the sweat from his brow as he worked. He carefully inspected the roof and placed new shingles in the spots where raindrops had found their way into the coop. Bill had a pack of cedar shingles on the roof, and about a half-pound of shingle nails in an old, red Prince Albert Crimp Cut tobacco tin. He was near the top of the coop's roof when the faint buzzing sound of an airplane reached his ears. Bill was so engrossed in his work that he did not pay any attention to the oncoming aircraft.

As Bill was bent over looking carefully at the roof, the pack of shingles and the nails began to quiver as the noise of the plane became increasingly louder. Bill turned and looked up toward the noise to see an airplane heading directly at him, at a height of about two hundred feet and bearing down.

Sensing his life was in danger, Bill immediately jumped off the roof, landing in the slop of a pig yard adjacent to the chicken coop. The pigs scattered, and the chickens, which had been scratching in the dirt around the coop, flew in all directions. As he lay there with his hands in the mud, Bill looked up to see Clem waving and laughing as the airplane rolled to an upside-down position and made a quick loop upward, taking off into the sky.

Bill's first reaction was to shake his fist at Clem, but instead he looked down at his mud-caked clothes and began to laugh.

"After he graduated from high school, Clem worked full time for a spell at a Sinclair gas station in the summer of 1929. His heart was not in his work there, as all he really wanted was to fly. He visited Mr. Davis to find out if there was any way he could work for Michigan Airways full time. Art could not take him on full time but let him know about an opportunity to work at the Luce County

Airport in Newberry, Michigan, for Sven Copenhagen," Margot explained. "I suppose you know that Newberry is in the Upper Peninsula of Michigan. After Art arranged for Clem to work for Sven, Clem drove up to Mackinaw City in a used 1926 Ford Model T he had recently purchased. From there he took the car ferry across to St. Ignace and made his way to the Luce County Airport."

I had crossed the majestic Mackinaw Bridge several times as a child vacationing in the UP. I guess I hadn't thought about a time before the bridge was in operation. It was fascinating for me to learn a little about Michigan from a foreigner. Margot continued to recount her story about Clem's time in the UP.

When the ferry docked in St. Ignace, Clem climbed into his car and drove it to the off-ramp and onto Michigan's Upper Peninsula. Clem had seen the UP from the air on some of his flights but had not actually stepped on any part of it. The air was so fresh and clean, unlike what he had experienced anywhere before. He drove to a nearby Zephyr gas station and had the gas tank filled and the oil and tires checked. He paid forty-eight cents for eight gallons of gasoline. He paid another two cents for a map of the UP and made his way to the Theodore Roosevelt International Highway. He started his fifty-seven-mile journey to the Luce County Airport along the southern coast of Michigan's Upper Peninsula. Clem was used to seeing Lake Michigan, Lake Huron, and Lake Erie from the sky on a regular basis. However, he had not traveled the coast by land along any of these lakes up to this point in his life. He stopped for a short time to sit on the beach. He took off his shoes and socks and walked a way along the beach, eating an apple while he watched the waves of Lake Michigan reach up the shoreline as far as they could go before returning to the lake, only to repeat this motion over and over. After about twenty minutes spent enjoying the water, Clem climbed back into his car to resume his journey.

Clem had virtually everything he owned in his car. His clothes were packed into an old suitcase given to him by his father Gottlieb. He had two sets of work boots and a pair of baseball cleats. He also packed his ball glove, his catcher shin guards, and his favorite Hillerich & Bradsby Company Louisville Slugger wooden bat. Louise, his step-mom, had made him some sandwiches, and he had a cloth sack filled with a dozen Northern Spy apples, which were not quite ripe and tasted tangy the way Clem liked them. He also had a canvas bag full of miscellaneous mechanic tools that he had acquired over the last three years. Clem was wearing his Sunday clothes, consisting of a white shirt and string tie with a checkered vest. His dark pants and black shoes completed his attire.

The road was rather rough in spots, the springs on Clem's Model T groaning and squeaking as he drove along some bumpy sections in the road. The sun shone bright, and Clem adjusted the brim of his Davis Airport cap to shade his eyes. After about thirty-five miles, Clem turned north onto Borgstrom Road. This stretch of road no longer provided him a view of Lake Michigan. Instead, it revealed a sparsely populated stretch of trees, trees ... and more trees. The first ten miles or so were beautiful to Clem, but as the road continued, the view seemed to be unchanged. He traveled through miles and miles of swampland filled with cedar trees. With few homes along the way, the journey became rather monotonous. When he finally reached M-28 to turn left for the airport, Clem was relieved to know that his journey was nearly at an end.

After turning west, Clem drove five miles and arrived at a three-by-five-foot wooden sign next to the road that read LUCE COUNTY AIRPORT. The sign had an arrow below pointing right toward a tree-lined two-track driveway. The sign had two supporting posts, one on each side, but was not attached on the right so that it slanted downward. Clem thought he would make a good impression before arriving at the airport office by straightening up the sign. He stopped his car, got out, and walked up to the sign through the tall weeds. When he lifted the right side of the sign to straighten it, it disconnected on the left and fell hopelessly to the ground. Clem did not have the tools to fix what he had accidentally destroyed, so he leaned the sign up against the posts on the ground. Most of the road sign was no longer visible in the tall weeds. Shaking his head, he muttered, "This is not a very good start to my new job."

Clem turned right and entered a two-track driveway leading to the airport. After about a quarter mile, the narrow road entered a wide expanse of open ground. He expected to see an airstrip similar to what he had experienced at Davis Airport, but what he found was very, very different.

On the right was an old gambrel-roofed barn. It needed a new coat of red paint and was in a state of much disrepair. An old airplane with the right wing dangling down to the ground was sitting next to the barn, anchored to ground tie-downs. A small house was visible next to the barn, which also needed much repair. There was a long, turf landing strip extending from the barn on an angle to the north and west. A large, red, metal tank on stilts with yellow letters, which read FUEL, was located to one side near the end of the airstrip. On either side of the runway was farm soil that had been tilled and prepped for planting. In the area north of the runway stood an elderly woman, an elderly man, and a mule with a pair of sacks of seed potatoes attached to a makeshift saddle horn hanging on both sides. The man had long, gray hair, a scruffy beard, and wore an old red-flannel shirt and overalls. The woman also had gray hair and wore a long light-blue dress. A bandana adorned her head, holding her hair back as she bent over to complete her planting task. They both appeared to be about seventy years old in Clem's estimation, and they had weathered skin. They were dropping the seed potatoes into a small crevice etched in the dirt, then covering them up with their bare feet in the loose soil. As Clem parked his Ford by the barn, the farm couple noticed his arrival and took the occasion to drop what they were doing and meet their guest. They walked slowly toward Clem to greet him.

"Hello," Clem said, starting the conversation as he drew near the old farm couple.

"Vell hello to you, young man," came a high-pitched, raspy response from the gentleman farmer. He immediately held out his soil-stained right hand and shook Clem's hand while putting his equally dirty left hand on Clem's right shoulder.

"My name is Sven, and dis here, she is Mama," Sven said, motioning to his wife. "And da mule, vy she's my Ol' Puddins. You like mules, aye?"

"My name is Clem … Clem Sohn. Art Davis told me to report here for a job. I'm just not sure how I feel about mules," Clem responded, looking Ol' Puddins over with a wary eye as she slowly, casually maneuvered behind him.

"Oh my, Ol' Puddins, she is an honest mule; I tink you'll like her," returned an excited Sven. "Mama and me, vee is gettin' a vee lil' tired of seedin' taters. You look like a strong young man, aye?"

"Well, I've done my share of farm work back home," Clem answered. As he spoke, Ol' Puddins stealthily made her way directly behind Clem and pushed him in the middle of his back with her muzzle. He lost his balance and lunged forward into Sven's arms.

"Ha! Looks like my Ol' Puddins vants to get back to plantin', aye?" Sven noted as he helped straighten Clem back up. "You go ahead now and start plantin' dem taters. Just go back to the lines vee left off and drop 'em in about ever' half foot. Be sure an' cover 'em up now, aye?" Sven explained, pointing to the open field.

"What about the planes?" Clem asked, not quite understanding what he had gotten himself into.

"Oh, don't you vorry now, dey'll be plenty far enough avay from you and Puddins if'n dey fly in," Sven responded. Sven turned toward Mama and began walking away, saying, "Maybe now I can straighten dat sign up front before she be fallin' down, aye?"

Clem raised his hand to stop Sven and tell him about the sign just as Ol' Puddins pushed him in the middle of the back again. Clem fell face-down in the dirt. He slowly got back up and brushed himself off. Sven was now some distance away, so Clem led Ol' Puddins by the halter to the area he had last seen Sven and Mama when he arrived. He found the row lines sketched in the dirt and began dropping and planting potatoes.

"So, Clem started working at the airport by planting potatoes?" I asked, amused by the predicament Clem had found himself in.

"Oh yes," Margot replied, laughing a bit. "Clem didn't know it at the time, but he would spend most of the summer and fall tending to those potatoes. Precious few airplanes actually landed at this remote airport at that time. Clem was a man of honor, and stayed with the Copenhagens until the potato harvest was completed out of respect for Art. But before the deep winter snows fell, he loaded up his Model T and headed back to Lansing."

As Margot finished her sentence, the thin, faint sound of a jet airliner could be heard overhead. The sound drew both of our attention, and we looked up to see a silver passenger jet flying westward over the cemetery.

"Wouldn't Clem have loved to see something like that big passenger jet?" Margot questioned. "He loved to fly, and he felt so at home in the sky."

"He never rode on a jet airliner?" I asked.

"No, no, Ren, jets weren't invented yet," Margot explained. "But if Clem had lived to a ripe old age, I'm sure that he would have piloted them."

I felt a little silly, like I should have known this based on the year Clem passed away. But then, I'd never done much reading about aviation history.

GROUND RUSH

"When Clem came back from Newberry in the fall of 1929, Art Davis had a job opening for him. Art added aerial racing to his stunt-flying pursuits and also became a WACO plane dealer," Margot said. "With these additions, there was a need for more help, and Clem fit the bill. Art took him on as a full-time airplane mechanic. Clem loved working for Michigan Airways. He got a chance to tinker with the plane bodies and their engines. He usually took them for flights when his repairs were completed to test-drive his work. He told me that this job was the most rewarding of his life."

"When did he start flying like a bat?" I asked, getting a little impatient to hear about this part of Clem's life. The ceremony was due to start in just over an hour.

Margot laughed as she sensed my exasperation. "In 1932 Clem started parachuting. There was not a lot known about parachuting at that time. Jumpers did not have much control of their flight and were primarily left to the variants of the wind to determine where they would eventually land. Clem started going with Art to air shows at that time to watch him race. He also began parachuting with a static-line jump team. It was at one of these shows that he first met Spud Manning."

Margot began telling the story of the life-changing meeting between these two aviators.

Clyde Ice was piloting a Ford Trimotor single-wing aircraft at the Cleveland Airshow on Saturday, September 3, 1932. Clyde was originally from South Dakota and, like Art Davis, was an avid aviator. Clyde traded two used cars to a farmer for an army surplus World War I Standard Curtis Trainer in 1919. This plane was badly damaged from the exploits of the war. Clyde repaired the engine and three major structural issues on the body. He then self-taught takeoffs and landings and became a truly experienced pilot. The Ford Trimotor he flew on this day thirteen years later was primarily used as a cargo plane. At this airshow, it carried a team of six static-line parachutists. They sat on small flip-down benches inside the fuselage on both sides as Clyde flew to the appropriate location to release the team. He was flying at an altitude of five thousand feet. Clyde knew the wind direction from the airfield tetrahedron and had released two jump dummies to see how the wind speed would affect the parachutists. Clyde had determined that releasing the parachutists about one thousand feet upwind of the target at the current altitude would carry the jumpers within a close proximity to the landing zone. There were about fifteen thousand people on the ground watching Clyde position the plane with great anticipation.

In static-line jumping, the ripcord for each parachute was connected to an overhead cable inside the aircraft. As each parachutist exited the plane, the ripcord was automatically pulled by the weight of the jumper, and the chute deployed almost immediately after they left the aircraft. Clem was third in line to step out of the airplane among this jump team. This was only Clem's ninth jump, and there were still a healthy number of butterflies in his stomach as he waited for the signal to exit the aircraft.

Clyde gave the parachutists the thumbs-up "go" signal, and the first parachutist opened the side door of the plane: first just a crack to decompress the fuselage, then all the way. When the door was safely secured open, he jumped out of the aircraft. The next parachutist jumped out seconds later, followed by Clem and the other three. These jumpers were all dressed in white, with black boots and brown-leather helmets. They also wore goggles to protect their eyes and keep them moist. Gloves were worn to keep their hands warm as they made their descent. The parachutes were made of white canvas. They were very visible in the near-cloudless sky.

After Clem jumped from the plane, his parachute quickly deployed. Clem looked from side to side to see how the other parachutists were faring. All of their chutes had successfully opened. He loved this feeling of drifting in the sky, far away from the noise of the aircraft. From his perch in the firmament, Clem could see for miles in all directions. The beauty of Lake Erie was astonishing to him. As his round parachute moved with the slight breeze, he could also see the city of Cleveland, the airfield, and the large crowd below. On this particular day, the winds were relatively calm and steady, and the calculations Clyde had made proved correct. All of the parachutists landed on the two-mile-long airfield. As Clem and the others waved to the audience and disconnected their gear, the airshow announcer Tom Manning from WTAM began to rev up the crowd, teasing the next jump by daredevil Spud Manning.

"Folks, let's give these jumpers a round of applause to let them know how much you appreciate them." The crowd gave a rousing applause to Clem and the other jumpers.

Tom continued, "Now that you've seen how parachuting is done, Spud Manning will treat you next to an amazing free-fall jump.

Folks, this astounding daredevil will jump out of the plane and fall eight thousand ... yes, that's eight thousand feet, before pulling his ripcord. There is no one like Spud in all of the world, folks! He will perform this death-defying feat before your very eyes."

The announcer vamped with other airshow announcements until Spud's plane had reached a height of about eight thousand feet. Without a parachute, Spud was not easily detected in the sky after jumping from the plane. To assist the audience viewing, Spud planned to leave a white streak of flour behind him as he made his descent. Tom was watching with binoculars and let the crowd know when he caught sight of Spud.

"Ladies and gentlemen, Spud has left the confines of the airplane, and I can see him falling now. He's approaching the ground at an amazing speed." The crowd was straining at first to see Spud. Spud reached down to a sack of flour attached to his left lower leg and poked a hole in it. As he descended, the flour left a trail behind him. Just then, the audience began to notice him and reacted enthusiastically. The announcer began to tease the crowd.

"Folks, Spud looks to be falling faster than usual. He should have pulled his ripcord by now ... could something be wrong? SPUD, PLEASE OPEN YOUR CHUTE!" The spectators began to feel uneasy as Spud maintained his fast descent. He drew closer now, five thousand feet and falling quickly; he began to twist and contort in the air, which was of great interest to the crowd. However, they could not tell if this was planned for the jump or if this represented some kind of problem.

"Oh Spud," Tom Manning implored, "PLEASE PULL THAT RIPCORD! Folks, this is not looking good! SPUD, IF YOU CAN HEAR ME ... OPEN YOUR CHUTE!"

Spud continued to fall another one thousand feet. The crowd became increasingly concerned, starting to yell advice at a feverish pitch. They were also anxious for Spud to pull his ripcord.

Tom continued his plea, "SPUD ... oh my ... SPUD, PLEASE,

PLEASE PULL YOUR RIPCORD!! This is very dangerous! SPUD … SPUD, WE DON'T WANT TO SEE YOU DIE!!"

Women began to wail as it looked like Spud would be dashed to the earth.

Traveling at nearly two hundred miles per hour, Spud fell another one thousand feet, and then another. At just over nine hundred feet above the ground, Spud stretched out his arms and legs to slow his descent slightly and then pulled his ripcord. As his parachute deployed, the crowd erupted in delirious applause. Clem and the other parachutists had wrapped up their chutes and were being carted off of the airstrip by a small truck, but no one noticed. All eyes were riveted on Spud. As he slowly made his way to the ground, Spud waved to the audience, which caused them to all shout and cheer for him. Spud was about to land one hundred fifty yards from the audience seating. Some in the crowd could not contain themselves and left the audience bleachers to run at Spud. By the time he landed, over one thousand members of the crowd were there to see the amazing daredevil up close. They screamed for him and patted him on the back, showing their extreme admiration for his near-death experience. They did not know that the announcer's bantering was previously planned out. Spud's jump went exactly as planned, and he was never in any danger, which the announcer knew full well. But this gave the crowd something to tell their friends to ensure that Sunday's spectator crowd was as large or larger.

"This highly emotional jump and landing did not go unnoticed by Clem," Margot noted. "As he watched Spud's landing and the admiration of the crowd, he wanted to be the daredevil that Spud was, longing for the adulation Spud received. In the course of the day, Clem caught up with Spud and engaged in a conversation with him about free-fall jumping. Spud was not willing to share the details of the moves he'd made while falling several thousand feet. Undaunted, Clem began to plan for an eventual free-fall jump of his own.

"In the spring of 1933, Clem started to learn free-fall jumping at Davis Airport. He told me it was exhilarating! He had Art take him up at ever-higher altitudes so that he could experiment while falling through the air. He learned that he could slow himself down in the free fall by extending his arms and legs. He also found that he could actually move somewhat laterally in the air by making a swimming motion with his body. He performed his first public free-fall jump at the Ionia Free Fair on August 14, 1933. During the week-long fair, Clem jumped several times.

"Clem began to free-fall jump with other parachutists. This caused ever more excitement for the crowds. It wasn't long before these parachuting madcaps developed a game of chicken of sorts. Together the jumpers would challenge each other to see who would be the first 'chicken' to pull their ripcord. This brought them ever-closer to the ground before their chutes deployed. There was one such event that didn't go at all well for a friend of Clem's."

In June of 1934, Clem made a parallel jump with fellow parachutist Jerry Wessling. This jump was at an airshow at the Floyd Bennett Airport in Brooklyn, New York. The two were set to play chicken at this airshow. Jerry was from Ohio but actually lived in the Lansing, Michigan, area for a time: the two of them became great friends. They each had over two hundred parachute jumps in their pasts and had become somewhat proficient at this skill. Jerry often won the prize money by landing closest to the flag at parachute events. The two enjoyed dinner the night before the airshow and teased each other about who would pull first on the following day. They also talked a little about "ground rush," specifically how they both knew instinctively when to pull their ripcords. During free fall, people feel as if they are floating, the earth seeming to remain at about the same distance below them. But somewhere under one thousand feet, the earth's surface suddenly rushes up at them, spreading out. This is known as ground rush, and it's considered a sign to pull the ripcord immediately. The more a person parachutes, the less ground rush affects them.

On this day they ascended together some eight thousand feet above the airfield in an army cargo plane, making final preparations for their jump by checking their belts and adjusting their goggles and gloves. They talked briefly about their future plans, and Jerry even mentioned that he was thinking of moving back to Lansing and working for Art Davis if there was enough work for him to do. Clem told Jerry that he hoped they could jump together at an upcoming airshow soon, and then they received the thumbs-up signal from the pilot to jump.

"Good luck," Clem said to Jerry, then jumped first out of the airplane.

Jerry yelled, "Good luck to you, too!" and quickly followed. They stayed somewhat close together as they descended toward the ground. They even locked arms at one point to let the crowd see they were descending at the same elevation.

"You look like a chicken," Jerry yelled at Clem as they descended together.

"I feel like an eagle," replied Clem with a big grin.

When they got to roughly nine hundred feet above the ground, Clem pulled his ripcord first. He felt that he had descended as far as he could safely plummet and was surprised at how many seconds it took before Jerry finally pulled his cord. Jerry had won this chicken battle; however, the canopy of his parachute was not able to fully inflate, because he had waited too long to pull his ripcord. A strong crosswind pushed Jerry sideways just as he landed, and his head hit the ground with incredible force. Jerry's leather helmet was not enough to protect him from this fall. Clem viewed Jerry's motionless body as he slowly descended to the ground. He knew something was wrong and wanted desperately to be by his friend's side. By the time Clem landed, had disconnected his parachute, and ran nearly one hundred yards to Jerry's side, an ambulance was already there, and Jerry was being strapped to a gurney. Clem jumped into the ambulance and rode nearly five miles with his unconscious comrade to the hospital. Jerry had a pulse but was otherwise listless and didn't respond to anything that was said.

Clem sat in a waiting room for two hours in his flight suit before finally learning from a physician that Jerry had died from a fractured skull. Clem was torn between feelings of anger at Jerry for not pulling his ripcord earlier to save his life, and feelings of deep remorse. He didn't like to see others take chances performing such dangerous free-fall jumps. Clem was deeply shaken by this accident, but performed his two hundred twelfth solo free-fall jump from fifteen thousand feet the very next day, confident in his ability to avoid danger. Clem was a pallbearer at Jerry's funeral the following week.

I was shaken by this terrible tragedy as Margot told it to me. It helped me to understand just how dangerous Clem's profession was. After a brief spell of silence, I flipped over a full page in my notebook, eager to learn more.

"So, was Spud the first batman?" I asked, trying to keep my facts straight.

"Heavens no, Ren," Margot exclaimed. "Spud simply landed with a normal parachute. What made Clem so special was that he developed wings."

"You mean he could fly?" I inquired.

Margot answered, "Not exactly, but he did believe that people would eventually be able to fly on their own. With that belief, Clem began to study the wings of bats to see how they were constructed. He wanted to make a set of wings that would allow him to glide horizontally in the sky after jumping from a plane. After one of his free-fall jumps at the Ionia Free Fair, he was hanging out with his family friends, Ed and Larry Motz. He drew a design for the wings in their presence, and the following year he made them."

"Are you sure this is going to work?" asked Art Davis as he helped strap on the wings that Clem had made.

"I'm certain it will," replied a confident Clem.

"Well, let's get you in the plane and find out," Art said nervously.

Art had set up a stepladder next to the back seat of his two-seater Waco biplane. He was not at all certain Clem could even sit in the aircraft while wearing the strange winged contraption he had developed. Clem slowly climbed the ladder with Art close behind. As he reached the top step, Clem grabbed the side of the plane's open cockpit and lifted his leg into the back seat. He then placed his other leg into the seat and squeezed his winged apparatus next to his body so that it fit into the passenger-seat area. He grabbed two handles on the front of the cockpit and slowly leaned back to sit down. His wings were a little long for sitting and pushed up into his armpits when he was seated.

"Are you all situated?" Art asked.

"I think so," Clem responded, "but I'm not going to be able to fasten my seat belt."

"That shouldn't be a problem," Art replied. "You aren't going to want to fuss with a seat belt when you jump. How *are* you going to jump, anyway?"

"Well, I'll have to sort of play that by ear this first time," Clem responded. "Don't worry, I'll be alright. If it feels like it isn't going to work, I may have to make some adjustments to the wings. But I think it will work."

Art set the ladder aside and climbed up onto the wing of the aircraft and into his front cockpit seat. He started the engines and leaned back, exhaling an anxious breath.

"You want to jump at five thousand feet, right?" he asked before moving down the runway.

"Yes, no more than that," came Clem's reply.

Art was a little skeptical but also very excited at the prospect of Clem's creation working. The airshows needed something new to draw in more people, and it did not escape him that this could be really big. The Great Economic Depression had begun in 1929, and businesses everywhere were feeling the financial pinch. Airshows were a godsend to Art, as they provided valuable revenue in a dismal time. It seemed that people everywhere wanted something to excite them, and regardless of their income, they found a way to afford a day at an airshow. If Clem could in fact fly, it would be a first and the talk of the country.

Art flew his aircraft upwind of the airstrip and rose to a height of five thousand feet. He turned to look at Clem, who was simply looking down, enjoying the view as he always did.

"It's time!" Art yelled back at Clem.

"Okay, I'm ready," Clem answered.

Clem then grabbed the two handles that had been so instrumental in getting him positioned in the cockpit and stood up in front of his seat. There was an immediate rush of air in his face and against his torso, pushing him back.

"Slow down as much as you can," Clem yelled at Art.

Art pulled back the throttle, which greatly slowed the flight. Clem then stood on his seat and let go of the left handle. With his right hand still holding on, he maneuvered his right leg out of the plane onto a small step used to enter and exit the cockpit. He then lifted his left leg out of the cockpit. His right leg slipped off of the step, and he was left dangling from the plane with his right hand still gripping the cockpit handle. Art could see Clem's difficulty and dipped the right wing downward so that the tail wings would not hit Clem when he let go. After this occurred, Clem let go of the handle and started his fall.

Clem's wings remained at his side as he reached down to feel the crude wooden paddles at the end of each wing. He grabbed them and began to open his wings. As soon as he did, he began twisting dizzily in the air, so he brought his arms back close to the side of his body. Still twisting, Clem decided to open just his right wing, which immediately stopped the twisting motion. He then ever so slowly began to let out the left wing. He was now in flight!

Clem could not believe the exhilaration he felt as he slowly went from a vertical fall to more of a horizontal position. He was actually flying! Art had turned his aircraft around and began circling Clem as he made his descent. Clem flew sideways for about one quarter of a mile, then slightly retracting his left wing he began to turn to his left. He then extended his left wing and slightly retracted his right wing, turning to the right. Clem was performing something he had only ever dreamed of doing: controlling his direction and pattern of flight. Clem closed his eyes and felt the air move over his body and his incredible wings. This was the most amazing feeling he had ever experienced. As he drew closer to the ground he decided to pull his ripcord at about two thousand feet to ensure that his parachute would clear his winged apparatus. His parachute deployed flawlessly and he made his slow descent to the ground. Art landed on the airstrip ahead of the young aviator he had mentored, beaming with pride at Clem's accomplishment. Clem would practice many more times that summer, and perfect all aspects of his winged descents. What Clem had accomplished was truly unique!

"So, he based the design of his wings on bat wings. Is that why they called him the batman?" I asked.

"I suppose it was," Margot replied. "After Clem jumped in his first set of wings in 1934 he was called many different names, like Batman, Birdman, Batwing Jumper, and the Human Bat. He was a real novelty, and began to develop a following. He jumped in numerous large cities in the United States, like: Detroit MI, Memphis TN, Chicago IL, Montgomery AL, New Orleans LA, Las Angeles CA, Davenport IA, New York NY, Daytona, Lakeland, Orlando, and Tampa FL.

"Clem's wings were initially made of canvas stretched over a steel tubing frame. This frame was designed to withstand the pressure of high speeds. It was fastened tightly to his chest and waist with common belts, and the wings were made to fold against his body when not in use. Small paddles made of wood were used to grab onto the ends of the wings to pull them from his side to an open position for flying. He also added a piece of cloth sewn between his legs that acted like the tail feathers of a bird. Others tried to mimic the design quite unsuccessfully, and several died trying to fly like Clem. He was indeed an amazing visionary. I would eventually get a chance to see and touch his amazing wings."

"How far could he fly with his batwings?" I asked, amazed at what Margot had revealed.

"Clem said he could fly horizontally for a mile or more, depending on how high he was when he left the aircraft," Margot noted. "He told me about a particularly impressionable jump he made in 1936 in London, England."

June 6, 1936 was a wonderful day in London England. It was warm and sunny, perfect for the London Airshow in Hyde Park. On this Saturday and the following Sunday, the skies would be filled with aerial displays of all sorts, from stunt flying to racing. There would be sky walking and parachuting as well. Among the daredevils featured in the show was the Batman, Clem Sohn. Clem was scheduled to make seven jumps over the two-day show, three on Saturday and four on Sunday.

There was much hype about Clem in the advertisements leading up to the show. News of his exploits had spread to Europe, and there was great interest in his daring aerial exploits. The crowds were expected to number over seventy thousand during the two-day event, and Clem was receiving much attention before and after each jump.

Clem experienced no problems with his jumps on Saturday. The announcers as always played up the danger involved in the daring turns and flips Clem performed during his descent. On Clem's sixth jump (his third that Sunday) he was falling to the ground at about 150 miles per hour and pulled his ripcord at just below one thousand feet. His right wing, which typically rested next to his body when he released the paddle at the end, remained extended and got caught in the lines of his main parachute. This did not allow his chute to fully deploy. Sensing the possible danger, Clem immediately pulled the ripcord on his secondary chute.

Two things saved his life that day. The first was his secondary parachute; the second was that he was lucky enough to land on the roof of a bystander's car. The car helped to soften the impact, but Clem still broke his arm and dislocated his shoulder in the fall.

"I suppose it would have been best for Clem if he had given up free-fall parachuting after his friend Jerry died, and then this close call," Margot said. "But Clem was not afraid. He felt that he had more to offer the world. He did not want to give up a chance to advance his theory of human flight."

"What did Clem do when he wasn't flying like a bat?" I asked.

"Clem was quite a prankster, and he told me a very funny story of one of his escapades," Margot replied after a moment's thought.

TRUCKLOAD OF WHAT?

"Once he began parachuting with his bat wings, Clem became quite a celebrity," Margot continued. "He was commanding a very good fee for his parachuting appearances ... upwards of several thousand dollars at each air-show. This was a lot of money for anyone, considering the United States was in the midst of the Great Depression. In spite of his fame, he didn't forget who he was or where he came from. He would often drive north from his home in Lansing to Fowler to visit with his longtime friends. On one such trip, he ran into an old nemesis ... Tank Thelen."

Clem Sohn traveled to Fowler on Saturday, August 15, 1936, to pick up a 1934 Ford Model 40 automobile he had purchased from his uncle John Kramer's Ford dealership. The Model 40 sported a flat-head V8 engine and was very fast. This model of Ford made history as the make of automobile the notorious outlaws Bonnie and Clyde had stolen and were killed in two years earlier.

Clem was no longer wearing the sling for his broken arm and

dislocated shoulder that he sported due to the mishap he'd had in England the previous June. Word spread that Clem was coming to town, and a gathering of some of his family and friends met him in downtown Fowler at Miller's Tavern that evening. When he journeyed to Fowler, it was common for Clem to acquire an audience who longed to hear of his travels and exploits. After taking possession of his car, Clem drove it a couple of blocks to Main Street and walked to the bar. An assembly of interested listeners was already seated at round tables scattered around the pub. Clem walked in and sat on a tall bar stool facing them, with his back to the fifteen-foot-long mahogany bar.

Clem's taste in clothing had changed significantly since making his splash in the world. When he wasn't working at Davis Airport, he dressed with style in spite of the nation's ongoing financial misery. On this day, when most in the tavern were dressed in drab-colored and well-worn clothing, he looked like a true American hero in his impeccable attire. Clem wore a long-sleeved white shirt with the sleeves rolled up above his elbows. He also sported a yellow necktie with a brown polka dot pattern and brown-leather suspenders buttoned inside his white pants. Brown and white saddle shoes with white laces completed his attire. Among the crowd on this day was his lifelong best friend Larry Motz, Larry's brother Ed Motz, Clem's brother Lefty with his wife Marion, and Rita Fields.

As the song *The Way You Look Tonight* (sung by Fred Astaire) played in the background from an RCA radio, Clem told a story related to one of his record-breaking jumps in Florida the year before. "… and I was so cold at an altitude of over fifteen thousand feet in the air," Clem told his fascinated audience, "that I decided to free fall downward as fast as I could just to get into some warm air. I was going over two hundred miles per hour straight down. I had the Atlantic Ocean on my right and Daytona Beach on my left."

When Clem finished making this statement, a lone, sarcastic

handclap could be heard from the back of the room by the bil-liard table. It was Tank expressing his mild disdain at the attention Clem received for his heroic tales. Tank still lived in neighboring St. Johns, but he occasionally made the trip to Fowler because he enjoyed bullying the "hicks," as he called them.

"And let me guess," Tank uttered loud enough for all to hear, "you pissed your pants and had to swap your nice white jump suit for a new one?"

After issuing this loud insult, Tank roared with laughter. The rest of the tavern remained silent.

"Why don't you get the hell out of here," Lefty said as he stood up from his chair and glared at Tank across the room.

Everyone in the tavern felt the same as Lefty save Doug Shook, who was sitting with Tank. Tank was well-known for his disre-spectful harassment of people, but Lefty and Clem had never been afraid of Tank's antics.

"What's the matter, doofus, does the truth about your baby brother embarrass you?" Tank retorted to Lefty.

"You're an ass!" Rita said, also looking at Tank. "Why don't you crawl back into your hole?"

Tank was clearly not in agreement with the crowd in the bar, and Doug and he were greatly outnumbered. Suddenly feeling very unwanted but not wanting to admit defeat, Tank responded:

"No problem, princess. This place is beginning to smell a little like a barn with all you fool farmers. Besides, it's about time you roll up the sidewalk for the evening." Tank erupted in solo laughter, again amused by his own abuse of Fowler and its townspeople.

"You may want to hit the can before you leave; you wouldn't want to piss YOUR pants on your way home," Clem exclaimed with a grin.

At this the saloon exploded in laughter as the bar patrons spent their nervous energy. Tank got up and made the long walk toward

Clem from the back of the bar. He stopped three feet away from Clem and wagged his thick finger at him.

"This isn't over, flyboy," he said in a somber tone.

Tank then stepped toward the door and caught his foot on a chair leg, stumbling and almost falling down. Everyone again burst into laughter as Tank caught himself on a nearby table.

"I think it is over, FALL-boy," Clem responded to the immense amusement of the bystanders.

Tank stood up straight and walked out of the pub without a look back, his friend Doug following nervously. He was mumbling something under his breath as he stepped over the threshold into the early evening air. Tank saw Clem's new blue Model 40 that he had heard him speak about earlier in the tavern. It was angle-parked on Main Street about a half-block north of Miller's tavern on the opposite side of the street.

Tank stopped Doug and said, "Do you feel like pushing that jerk's car up the street?"

"Let's push it into the big puddle next to the railroad tracks," Doug responded, pointing to a large area next to the tracks still flooded by recent rains.

Tank and Doug made their way to Clem's car. This was the time just before dusk when the storefronts were closed, but the evening bar crowd had not yet come into town. It was dinnertime for most, and there was no one walking on Main Street. Doug got inside Clem's unlocked car, released the parking brake, and took it out of gear. Tank was a large man and easily pushed the car away from the curb and continued pushing it backwards north away from the tavern toward the puddle about forty yards away. When they got it to the edge of the water, Doug hopped out and helped Tank give it a good push into the puddle so that the car was completely surrounded by water.

"This should fix that doofus," Tank said as he strode away, feeling rather pleased with himself. Doug and Tank jumped into

Tank's 1927 Series AA Chevrolet sedan and headed toward St. Johns.

The conversation in the tavern continued. Clem and his cohorts were beginning to feel high from running Tank out of town, not to mention the Stroh's beer they were consuming from longneck bottles. At about 8 p.m., Eldred Kramer, another relative of Clem's, walked into the tavern and asked, "Who's car is that in the mud puddle?"

Lefty got up and went to the door with Eldred. They looked to the north, and Lefty recognized his brother's new car resting in the middle of the water.

"Clem, come here," Lefty said, standing just outside the doorway of the bar.

Clem got up and went to the door. He grunted as he saw the location where Tank and Doug had ditched his car.

"That's got to be Tank's work," Clem muttered.

Clem had the car keys in his pocket as he walked out of the tavern and made his way to his vehicle with Lefty and Eldred. Before they made it to the car, Larry and Ed Motz had also left the tavern and followed them. Fortunately, the Model 40 had a rather substantial running board on the side, which was not covered in water. Clem made an athletic jump across three feet of water to the passenger side running board, opened the passenger door, and slid onto the driver's side without stepping in the water. He put the key into the ignition, set the spark to full retard, and depressed the starter button with his foot while pulling on the choke. The engine started immediately, and Clem pushed in the choke and advanced the spark before putting the transmission into gear to drive out of the water. There was no harm done to any of the car's components; however, these young men had a strong desire to retaliate for Tank's disrespectful deed in a way that might persuade him to avoid such actions in future.

"Do you have your pickup in town?" Larry asked his brother Ed.

"No, it's at home. Why do you ask?" Ed responded.

"Well, I was thinking that it would be fun to hook it up to Tank's car and pull it out of St. Johns and into the country," Larry explained. "That would get his goat!"

"I'm afraid we couldn't use it even if it was in town," Ed responded. "It's full of horse shit from cleaning out the barn. I was going to take the manure over to Grandpa's to put it in his garden, but I haven't been able to get over to his house yet."

"Wait," Clem exclaimed, "did you just say you have a truckload of horse manure?"

"Yes, that truck is so loaded the mainsprings have almost bottomed," Ed responded.

"Well, what if St. Johns starts smelling like a barnyard, too?" Clem asked.

"What do you mean?" Lefty questioned.

"How about if we get a few shovels and drive that truck to St. Johns and make it harder for Tank to get into his car than it was for me to get into mine?" Clem said with a wink.

That comment seemed to put everyone on the same page.

"Jump in my car with me, and I'll take you all to Ed's to get his truck," Clem said.

Larry, Lefty, Ed, and Eldred all squeezed into Clem's car for the five-mile trip into the country to Ed's house. When they got there, Ed ran into the house to get his keys while the rest scoured the outbuildings for pitchforks and shovels. Soon, Ed and Eldred were heading east toward St. Johns with the rest of the crew following in Clem's car. However, Clem was careful not to follow too close due to the smell of the cargo that Ed was hauling.

When they got to St. Johns, they parked on Brush Street, one block west of Clinton Avenue. Clinton Avenue was the main street in town, beginning at the courthouse on State Street and running directly north out of St. Johns. On that street was Tank's favorite hangout, Bruno's Bar. As the group suspected, Tank was in the bar, and his car was angle-parked across the street. Clinton Avenue was not a flat street. It gradually declined from its most southern point toward the north. When they saw Tank's car, Lefty hatched a plan.

"Let's push Tank's car north away from all of the other parked cars on the street," Lefty suggested. "Then we can really do a job on it with the horse shit."

The idea sounded good to all, so Lefty jumped into Tank's car to unfold the plan. He released the parking brake and took the car out of gear, then motioned for the rest to give it a push. After easing the car just a few feet backward, it quickly got away from the crew because of the street's downhill slant. As Tank's car rolled north-ward, the rest of the group ran to Ed's truck to bring the manure and complete the chicanery.

Lefty kept Tank's automobile in the southbound lane going backward about fifty yards down the street until it stopped unex-pectedly between the railroad tracks. These were the same tracks that ran through Fowler, just nine miles farther west. Before Clem and the others could make their way to Lefty, the blare of a train horn could be heard. The horn's familiar pattern (two long toots followed by one short toot and one final long toot) gave the resi-dents of St. Johns notice that the train was one quarter mile east of the crossing on Clinton Avenue. When the instigators heard this and saw from a distance that Tank's car sat on the tracks, they immediately panicked.

Lefty jumped out of the car and began trying to push it off the tracks to the north. But because the front tire sat in between the tracks, he was unable to move the car. Ed raced his truck around the corner, parked, and ran to Lefty to help out. The train horn blared again as the conductor sent a second signal to let people know the train was entering city limits. The rest of the guys also jumped from Ed's truck and ran to Tank's car and gave it a big push. With just seconds to spare, they were able to move the car off of the tracks and get themselves out of the way of the oncoming locomotive. Clem and his group of pranksters sat on the ground on the north side of the tracks panting as the train cars rolled by, one by one. They realized just how close they had come to the disaster of Tank's car getting demolished by a train. The hoax they were planning somehow didn't seem so important anymore.

As the caboose came into view and passed harmlessly by them, there stood Tank and Doug on the other side of the tracks, glaring daggers at Clem and his band of mischief-makers.

"You guys are sure a bunch of doofuses," Tank exclaimed. "If that train would have hit my car, I'd have sued all of your asses for everything you own. I'd see to it that you all rotted in jail for wrecking my car."

Tank's bold statements (after he had earlier pushed Clem's car into the water) suddenly gave Clem and his partners a renewed longing to retaliate.

"Well, that was a pretty mean trick you pulled on me with my car," Clem said.

"I didn't push your old rust bucket into the water," Tank exclaimed.

"Who said anything about water?" Lefty asked.

At this, Tank realized he had inadvertently given himself away as the perpetrator of the prank against Clem in Fowler. Not wanting to belabor the issue, he walked boldly across the tracks toward his car.

"Get away from my car, you dirt bags," Tank erupted. "Don't ever let me catch you by my car again or you'll be eating a knuckle sandwich!"

Clem and the gang moved swiftly from Tank's car. After a final moment of glaring, Tank and Doug climbed inside and drove off.

About two hours later, Clem, Lefty, Ed, Larry, and Eldred showed up in Miller's tavern again. But when they stepped inside, there was a distinct farm smell in the air. Clem's nice white pant bottoms and saddle shoes were stained with horse manure, as were the pants and shoes of the others with him.

They laughed and partied until the tavern closed as they told the bar crowd about their recent escapades in St. Johns.

"How did they get so stained with horse manure?" I asked.

"Well, let's just say Tank had quite a surprise waiting for him the next morning," Margot said, a little twinkle in her eye.

"Thaddeus, Thaddeus dear, come down here at once," Tank's mother, Laura, bawled into the second-floor stairwell.

"Aw, Mom, can't you just leave me alone? It's Sunday," Tank asked without moving a muscle in his warm bed. He was feeling slightly hung over from the frivolities of the night before.

"I think you'd better take a look out your window, dear," Laura suggested.

At this Tank's eyes bugged wide open, and he sat up in his single bed. Leaning to his left side, he pulled the curtain back to look out the upstairs window to the driveway below. What he saw was a rather large pile of horse manure, with the front and back of his car jutting out of it on opposite ends.

"I hate those Sohn doofuses!" he moaned quietly as he pulled the covers back over his head.

Margot began to laugh as she explained what had happened. "You see, Clem and the boys followed Tank at a safe distance all the way to his home just three miles outside of town. After Tank was safely inside, the guys quietly coasted up next to his parked car and shoveled out the horse manure next to Tank's car on both sides. Tank didn't even know this had occurred until the next morning."

"Did Tank ever retaliate for what Clem and his friends had done?" I asked.

"I don't think so," Margot responded. "You see, Tank really didn't have many friends, as you might expect. He knew that reprisal would only bring more back on him. He would not be able to match what Clem and his friends were capable of."

"Did Clem ever see Tank again?" I inquired.

"I'm unsure," Margot replied. "Clem never mentioned another instance of Tank to me. He would make fewer trips to Fowler going forward, as his involvement in parachuting and airshows began consuming all his time."

SMITTEN

"I sure laughed with Clem when he told me about the horse manure. He liked to gad about, for sure," Margot exclaimed.

"Can you tell me about the time you spent with him?" I asked.

"It started out quite strangely," Margot responded. She paused for a moment, as if bracing herself, then began recounting her memories of a trip that would be like no other.

Margot arrived at the New York harbor by taxi at about 10 a.m. on April 4, 1937. The harbor was filled with excited travelers boarding the Queen Mary cruise ship for a five-day trip across the Atlantic. This ship was a part of the Cunard-White Star Line, which carried passengers from New York to Southampton, England, then on to Cherbourg, France, before sailing back again. The Queen Mary was named in honor of the wife of King George V. It was over one thousand feet long and could accommodate more than two thousand passengers traveling at a speed of about thirty-five miles per hour. The vessel had been in service for less than a year, and the cabins and ship amenities showed little wear from tourist activity. The Queen Mary had wonderful facilities for the passengers to enjoy, including swimming pools, libraries, a music hall, beauty salons, and a grand dining hall. There was telephone service to anywhere in the world, and a colossal Atlantic Ocean map mural in the dining hall that continually showed the ship's progress along her journey.

Margot was heading back to England after a rousing two weeks of performances with the Britain Royal Ballet in New York City. The troupe had danced at the Capitol Theatre, which was just north of Times Square. The theater was lavishly decorated with gold-painted pillars and decorative carvings; it had a tall burgundy-colored curtain and a wonderfully large stage area, providing ample opportunity to take long run-ups for some of the more intense ballet movements. The crowds were fantastic, offering lengthy standing ovations each night. The afterglow parties were filled with entertainers from the United States, as well as politicians and other dignitaries who had been present at the performances. The show schedule was grueling; although the dance troupe was incredibly tired, they were satisfied with the experience. They had traveled to America by ship and were looking forward to the relaxation allowed by the lengthy return trip.

A group of female dancers from the ballet troupe was standing together on the dock with many news reporters moving about them, taking pictures and asking questions. Margot was dressed in a calf-length navy-colored skirt, knee-high sheer hosiery made of silk, a light-tan jacket over a black and white flowery blouse, and a silk pink neck scarf. She wore flat-heeled shoes that gave her feet and legs relief from the ballet slippers she wore during ballet practices and performances. The reporters were asking their final questions of the troupe before they embarked up the wide gangplank to enter the ship. Margot enjoyed the attention that she received from the U.S. news writers. It was flattering to be given so much notice by people in the states.

"Miss Fonteyn," a reporter said to get her attention, "what is it like to dance the role of Odette in Swan Lake?"

She was about to answer when another reporter about twenty feet away yelled out, "It's the batman!"

With that, all of the reporters abruptly left and ran toward a tall, young man walking toward Margot and the dance troupe. There was really nothing special about this gentleman, yet Margot could not take her eyes off of him. She asked the dancers standing by her if anyone knew who he was and why he commanded so much attention, but no one knew. She rather resented the fact that the special attention she was receiving had so rudely and suddenly ended.

The gentleman stopped just a few paces from the troupe and began to address the reporters, who were eager to get pictures and statements from him. He was tall and thin at six foot two inches. He was dressed in a black suit coat over a white shirt and a light-blue tie. He sported black pants and black shoes that were spit-shined. He carried a couple of abnormally large canvas bags, which seemed a little odd to Margot. As he spoke to the reporters, he looked her way, and they made direct eye contact. He kept his eyes on Margot for an unusual amount of time before she turned her head and made her way toward the footbridge with the rest of the dancers.

After taking a few steps, Margot turned back to look at this young man again. He was still regarding her intently while speaking with the press. At his side was a young woman with dark hair and a thin athletic build, who was somewhat attractive. By this time, there was a rather large swarm of newspaper reporters surrounding him, and he stood still, responding to the many questions that were barked at him. Margot had a strange feeling in her heart when she reached the first deck on the ship and presented her ticket. She wondered where he was staying, and if she would see him again as they traveled together on the ship.

"Did you get a chance to spend a lot time with him?" I asked. The answer to this question seemed a little obvious, but I asked it none-theless.

"Oh yes, indeed I did, Ren," Margot replied. "I was introduced to him formally that very evening, and our lives were never the same afterwards."

Margot continued her story of this special trip to Europe.

The ship left the harbor at about 3 p.m. that afternoon. By that time, the other dancers and Margot had found their tourist class cabins on the B Deck near the ship's stern. Margot was assigned a cabin with Gwyneth Mathews, who was a prominent dancer in one of the dance productions. Gwyneth was one of the shortest dancers in the troupe at about five feet in height. She had light-brown hair with brown eyes and a petite yet athletic build. She had a beautiful smile and a wonderful, easygoing personality, which helped to assure Margot her trip home would be a pleasant one. They stowed their gear in their cabin and freshened up a bit before taking a turn about the ship. The rolling waves were four feet high and con-tinually collided with the starboard side of the vessel as it began its trek eastward toward England. But aboard, there was virtually no sway or surge motions as a result. The sky ahead looked fore-boding, with dark, roiling clouds, and the wind seemed to grow stronger as the day progressed. By 6 p.m., a light rain began to fall.

The passengers did not know it at the time, but they would not see sunshine again until after the ship docked in England.

As the rain began to increase, Gwyneth and Margot entered the center of the C deck and made their way to the dining hall. The dining hall was located in the middle of the ship, both by length and height, and had eleven-foot ceilings. It was a long, rectangular room, about sixty feet wide by one hundred feet in length, and was very clean and extravagant. The walls were bright and shiny with chrome and mirrors. The chairs were of sycamore wood and upholstered in autumn red. The floor was a repeating pattern of two-feet-square tan marble tiles with dark- brown veins. Ten round tables (seating six people each, with bright-white tablecloths) lined the starboard side of the hall. Fifteen rectangular tables seating six people each lined the port side of the room. There were also three private dining rooms on both the starboard and port sides available for large group events. The table settings were of polished silver properly placed in front of each chair for formal dining. On the wall in the middle of the hall on the starboard side was a large tapestry painting by Phillip Conrad depicting scenes from the English countryside. Waiters dressed in white shirts with black bow ties, black pants, gold jackets with black lapels, and black leather shoes wandered the dining area seeing to the pleasures of every diner. Gwyneth and Margot went to the concierge station and waited to be seated.

The concierge was an elderly gentleman dressed much like the waiters, with one distinct difference: He had black epaulets on his shoulders surrounded by gold fringe. He wore a gold name tag on his lapel, which read *Kendall*. His silver hair and heavy mustache gave him a stately look, and he appeared to be anxious to see to their needs.

"Welcome ladies. I have the distinct pleasure of seating you. Would you care to dine alone, or with other guests?" he asked ever so politely.

Margot had never been one to shy away from meeting new people, so she responded, "We would like to meet some of the other passengers."

They followed the concierge to a table on the far side of the room. As they approached, they could see an elderly couple and the backs of what appeared to be a younger couple. The concierge stopped and pulled out two adjacent chairs at the table. The young gentleman positioned next to Margot turned and politely stood up until their new guests were seated. This gentleman and his lady friend were the ones the news reporters had flocked around at the harbor. When Margot saw his face, her body shivered uncontrollably for a split second, something stirring inside her at this surprise happenstance.

The young man had not changed his attire from the dock, but his guest had changed into a formal long dress which was rose colored. It was gathered at the waist and covered her torso to her neck, but the back had a V cut from just above her waist to her shoulders, exposing the milky skin of her back. It did not go unnoticed by Margot that this woman was wearing a wedding ring, and she made the seemingly obvious assumption that the young couple was married.

The older couple across the table was dressed in expensive clothing. He wore a black tuxedo over a white silk shirt with a bow tie and a black cummerbund. His shirtsleeves protruded from the ends of his jacket to expose gold cufflinks affixed with a black letter "B" in the center. He was short and overweight, with a high receding hairline and gold-rimmed glasses. He appeared to be in his late seventies. His guest was small in stature and wore a light-blue formal dress, with long sleeves and small glittering beads dispersed across her chest. Her hair was silver, and she wore dark-rimmed glasses. They both sported well-worn wedding rings as well.

"Good evening," the young gentleman began. "My name is

Clem, and this is Rhoda." He motioned to the provocatively dressed woman sitting at his right. Rhoda nodded her head to acknowledge the introduction.

"And I'm Tyler, and this here is my wife Adelle. We're the Burks, from Madison, Wisconsin," the elderly gentleman noted. He appeared to be a bit inebriated, sitting behind a glass of scotch on the rocks. His wife nodded slightly and took a sip of her white wine after raising her glass toward the young ladies.

"I'm Gwyneth, and this is Margot," Gwyneth responded in kind.

"Are you heading home?" Clem asked, noting the English accents.

"Yes," Margot replied. "We have just finished two weeks of ballet performances in New York and are eager to get back to London."

"What is the name of your dance company?" Rhoda asked.

"We are with the Britain Royal Ballet," Margot answered.

"I have never seen a ballet performance," Clem expounded. "How long have you been dancing?"

"I have been dancing for seven years," Gwyneth noted.

"… and I for thirteen," Margot added.

"You look too young to have danced for thirteen years," Rhoda stated.

This comment did not sit well with Margot, as she thought of herself as a grown woman. She smiled courteously at Rhoda, but it was difficult to do so.

Gwyneth added, "Margot is the star of our dance troupe. She is becoming well known throughout the world for her lead roles. To say her dancing is amazing is an understatement."

At this, Margot swelled with pride. She tried not to show it, nervously grasping her water glass and taking a rather large drink.

"Why are you traveling on this ship?" Gwyneth asked, looking at Clem.

"We are here on our honeymoon," Tyler responded out of turn, eager to be included in the conversation. "We have been married for fifty years come April 30th …"

"… April 29th," Adelle quietly corrected.

"Fifty years? Why that is fantastic," Clem said. "That deserves a toast! To the Burks," he said, raising his glass.

At Clem's pronouncement, everyone at the table raised their glasses and began clinking them together in a polite sign of unity. As she drew her glass back to take a sip of her dinner water, Margot looked to her right at Clem and noted that he was looking at her as well. He was so handsome to her, and she found herself wishing he were single.

Realizing that Gwyneth's question to Clem had not yet been answered, Margot once again queried, "Why are you going to England, Clem?"

Clem loved to speak about his passion and responded, "I am a performer like you, but I jump out of airplanes for a living."

This was somewhat confusing to the guests at the table, which Clem had anticipated. Seeing the inquisitive looks he was receiving, Clem continued.

"I am a bat-winged flyer. I jump out of planes wearing a special flying suit of my own design. I glide through the air like a bat, making loops and turns. When I get close enough to see the faces in the crowds, I pull the ripcord on my parachute and softly drift to the ground."

This new bit of information fascinated Margot. She twisted her napkin in her lap as she asked, "Isn't that dangerous?"

"Actually, I feel as safe in the air as you would in your grandmother's kitchen," Clem replied. This was a response that Clem had used often when asked this question.

"How long have you been doing these stunts?" Gwyneth asked.

"I don't consider myself a stuntman," Clem responded. "I am an aviator and am in total control of my flight movements at all times.

I feel like birds must feel when I'm gliding to the earth. I've been performing in this way for about three years."

"Clem is the very best at what he does," Rhoda interjected. "He has seen others try this and fail badly. He has seen some of them die. But he is the best!"

Clem continued, "I won't sit here and say that there is no danger to flying in this manner, but I will say that if you pay attention to what you are doing, you can greatly reduce the likelihood that there will ever be a problem."

"Have you never come close to death?" asked Tyler, who had also become very interested in the conversation.

"Well, I did have an accident last year in England at London's Gatwick airport," he explained, turning toward Margot. "I was about eight hundred feet above the ground when I pulled my ripcord. My right wing did not fold back against my body as it should have when I let go of it, and it got caught in my parachute. I saw my chute was not going to open, so I immediately pulled the ripcord on my auxiliary chute. It slowed my fall enough to save me."

"Oh dear," said Margot, "did it hurt when you hit the ground?"

"I didn't actually hit the ground ... I landed on an Englishman's car," Clem replied. Then, switching to an English accent, he continued, "The owner came up to me and said, 'Hey chap ... do you know you landed on my car?!!' to which I replied, 'No chap ... but do you know where I can find a good doctor?!!'"

At this everyone at the table began to laugh.

"I broke my arm and dislocated my shoulder on that jump, Margot," Clem said after the laughter died down.

"This is more dangerous than Clem is letting on," Rhoda chimed in. "One time in Miami, Clem landed successfully on the airstrip. A large army carrier was set to take off, and the suction from the propellers pulled Clem's open parachute toward the plane. Fortunately, the airport grounds crew ran out and grabbed the chute before he got caught in the props."

"I'm glad they showed up, because I wasn't quite ready to join the army," Clem said with a smirk on his face.

Again, the table erupted in laughter. Margot was quite smitten with Clem. She had never met anyone who was simultaneously so brave, so funny, and so likable.

"I'm on pins and needles at every airshow," Rhoda said. "I can't relax until the last flight is finished."

"How many jumps have you made?" asked Adelle, joining the conversation.

"I'm not really sure of the exact number," Clem replied, "but between the practice jumps and the performance jumps, it is well over two hundred."

"That's amazing!" exclaimed Gwyneth.

"I think you're amazing," replied Clem. "I can't imagine being able to dance on the tips of your toes. How in the world can you balance with such a small amount of your foot touching the floor?"

"It's not easy," Margot replied, "and it does start to hurt after a while. But I can feel energy from the audience, which keeps me focused and makes the hurt worthwhile."

"Touché!" replied Clem. "I get that. There is nothing like people coming up to you after a performance and telling you how much they enjoyed what you've done."

Three young girls approached the table and stood next to Clem. They appeared to be sisters by their nearly identical clothing. They were each wearing sweaters over dresses that were mid-calf in length. They also wore flats over white socks.

"Mr. Sohn, would you please sign our autograph books?" asked the tallest of the three.

"Of course, miss, what would you like me to write?" Clem responded.

"Oh, could you please write *To Rhylie*?"

Clem took hold of the autograph book and began to write.

"How do you spell Rhylie?" Clem asked.

"It's R H Y L I E," Rhylie responded.

"There you go," Clem said, handing the book back. "And how about you?" he said to the second girl while reaching out for her autograph book.

"Please write *To Paisley*," she said sheepishly to Clem.

"Okay, I think I can spell that one … like the pattern, right?" Clem asked with a smile as he took her book from her hand. She nodded to Clem in agreement.

The third lady was noticeably younger than the other two. Clem turned to her and asked, "What would you like me to write to you?"

She stood there speechless, too shy to respond. Seeing her hesitate, Rhylie spoke on her behalf.

"Please write *To Hadley*, H A D L E Y."

"That's a pretty name, Hadley," Clem said as he wrote in her book.

When he handed Hadley's book back to her, he asked, "Now tell me a little about yourselves."

Rhylie spoke up, saying, "We are sisters. We live on a farm near Wolfeboro, New Hampshire. Our father is a doctor there. We saw you at the New York airshow last year and can't believe we are actually speaking with you now."

"I'm nothing," Clem responded. "The real performers are these two ballerinas sitting next to me. They are from England. Wouldn't you like their autographs, too?"

"I don't think so," Rhylie responded, looking at the dancers and shaking her head. "It's been wonderful meeting you, and thanks for the autographs," she added before turning and retreating with her sisters to their table some distance away.

There was an awkward silence among the group for a few seconds. Then Margot said, "A batman has top billing over a ballerina any day!"

"I think they're just ignorant of ballet like I am," Clem responded.

"It was so nice that Clem tried to soothe me after I was rejected like that," Margot noted. "He could tell I looked nark."

"Nark?" I asked.

"Yes, you know, I was in a bad mood," Marot explained.

"Did Clem ever get a chance to see you dance?" I asked.

"Yes, he did, but it did not start out like you might imagine," Margot responded.

THERE'S BEEN A MISTAKE

"T"he weather on our trip to England continued to be rainy and windy," Margot noted. "The sea turned rougher each day, and we steadily got behind schedule as the winds were strong from the east. People increasingly got sick from the constant slow pitching of the ship. Some evenings, the wind would subside and provide temporary relief. On one such night, I made my way to the ship's music room to brush up on my dance."

"Were you sick from the ship's motion?" I asked.

"Some people have sea legs and aren't bothered so much by the waves. I must be one of them, because it didn't really affect me," replied Margot.

Smoothing her periwinkle dress over her knees, she then picked up on the story she had started.

The rain steadily fell on the ship on the third night of their voyage, but the wind had died down almost completely. The Queen Mary was very tranquil as she continued on her journey. Margot had danced earlier in the day with several members of the troupe, including Gwyneth, Elizabeth Miller, Mary Honer, and Fredrick Ashton. Frederick choreographed the dance creation called *Carnival,* and also performed the role of *Pierrot.* He thought it would be good to practice with the motion of the ship so that the dancers gave more thought to their every movement. Elizabeth Miller danced the role of *Columbine* in the *Carnival* ballet production. Margot was her understudy for this presentation. It was very important for each major dance role to have an understudy in ballet, as the intense movements subjected the dancers to injury. Margot had been remarkably free of injury in her career. She seemed to be created by God to dance and was very strong and reliable.

Although she had spent over two hours earlier in the day working on the *Carnival* production, she felt compelled to go back to the music room by herself to work on her steps for the *Les Patineurs* dance production. This shorter performance was also choreographed by Frederick and was performed on the same night as *Carnival.* Margot danced with Robert Helpmann in a difficult *pas de deux,* which was the third act of this performance. Margot had a complicated series of steps about one minute into the act, and was having difficulties transitioning through them. Her difficulty started at a point where Robert released her from a lift in front of him. Then she was spun on one toe in front of him for five turns, followed by four double-tours and then a series of grand jetés in a large circle around the stage. Margot was exasperated with the leaps, as they did not attain the height she was seeking. Leaping was not a strong suit in her dance, and she wanted desperately to improve this part of her performances.

Margot entered the music room, which was a large, open space about twenty feet square. The room had fifteen-foot ceilings made of horsehair plaster painted white. It was crisscrossed with a pattern of square, dark, wooden frames throughout, which protruded four inches down. The walls were also of plaster, decorated with hand-painted murals of scenes from New York City. Crystal sconce lights of an elegant French seashell design inside brass holders seven feet from the floor and five feet on center lined the entire perimeter. Each wall had its own dimmer switch to set the proper mood for the use of the room. The floor was entirely of natural colored white oak tongue and groove. White oak had been used in ship production in early American history, and was very hard and durable. There were about thirty wooden chairs in the room; these were set off to one side in stacks of six, leaving ample area in the center of the room for dancing. A Kraftone electric record player was brought into the room by the dance troupe the day before and had been left there for future use. There was also a collection of 78-rpm records containing music from the various ballet shows currently in production, played by the London Philharmonic Orchestra.

Margot was adorned in one of her pink recital leotards under an actor's robe. She changed from her flats into her ballet slippers, discarded the robe, and began to stretch her muscles for the tasks she would soon ask them to do. She then found the music for the *pas de deux*. Margot turned on the player and set the arm on the record about one-half inch inside the start of the music. As the music played, she walked to the center of the floor. At the appropriate moment in the song, she began her dancing with a series of grand jetés.

Outside, Clem was walking toward the bow of the ship on the starboard side under the metal awning, which covered the inside four feet of the second deck. The rain was coming down quite hard on this otherwise calm evening. It was a little chilly, so he reached up to button the top of his black woolen overcoat and pulled on the brim of his fedora. As he made his way forward, he detected the slight sound of music up ahead. In a matter of twenty seconds he was standing next to a closed door behind which the music emanated. Curious, he gently turned the doorknob and opened the door a crack to see what was going on.

Inside, he beheld Margot leaping and twirling in what was the most beautiful dance he had ever seen. As Margot made her consecutive leaps around the floor, Clem silently entered and stood next to the wall, undetected by Margot.

When Margot finished her last leap, she followed it with a series of single pirouettes, followed by a finish to the ballet fourth position. The music continued, but she stopped and walked toward the record player to repeat the process. When she lifted the arm on the player, a single clapping of applause drew her eyes to Clem.

Her body once again shivered for a split second, as it had when she first met Clem. There was something about this young man that caused a stir deep within her. She switched off the turntable and turned toward Clem.

"That was beautiful!" Clem announced after finishing his applause.

"Why, thank you very much, sir," Margot returned as she gave him a professional curtsy. "What brings you here?"

"I decided to make a pass around the ship before settling in for the night," said Clem. "It was very much worth the trip to see you perform." Clem walked across the room toward Margot.

"I think you are showing how little you know about ballet," Margot replied. "This is certainly not my best performance."

"I'll admit I know virtually nothing about your craft, but that was the most beautiful exhibition of dance I've ever seen," Clem replied, coming to a halt a few feet from Margot. His eyes glittered.

"Don't take on so … you don't know what you're looking at," Margot explained with a half-hearted laugh.

"I want to know," exclaimed Clem. "Can you tell me why you aren't pleased?"

"I have an awful time getting height on my leaps no matter how hard I try," Margot lamented.

"Can you show me what you mean?" Clem asked.

"Give me your coat and hat," Margot said.

Clem took off his coat and handed it to Margot along with the hat he was wearing. Margot took these items and set them down near her discarded robe. She then walked back to the center of the room and stood in front of Clem, facing away from him. She said, "Take hold of my waist."

Clem reluctantly placed his hands on each side of her body, just above the waistline.

"Now, lift me up as high as you can," Margot said.

Clem lifted Margot up high. He was astounded by how hard her muscular body felt, and how wonderful it was to hold her. Margot was also impressed by how easily Clem lifted her up: She enjoyed the feeling of being under his control.

"Now let me down slowly," Margot instructed.

Clem let her down ever so slowly. Margot stepped forward and then began her routine of four double-tours. When these steps were completed, Margot moved in a large circle, making a series of grand jetés in front of Clem. Clem was overwhelmed with emotion as he watched Margot dance so elegantly. She finished her last leap and landed in front of Clem at the precise location from which she had left. She then turned toward Clem and stopped, staring up into his eyes. This was the progression of the dance in *Les Patineurs*, but Clem thought it was an invitation to kiss Margot. He gently pulled her toward him and closed his eyes. This was not what Margot expected, and she reached out and slapped Clem on the left cheek with her strong, right hand.

Clem immediately let go, backed away, and said, "Margot, I am so sorry!"

Margot was both flattered and disturbed at what Clem had tried to do.

"I'll not play rumpy-pumpy with a married man!" Margot exclaimed.

"Married man??" Clem asked. "Whatever gave you that idea?"

"I saw the wedding ring on Rhoda's finger," Margot replied. "You'll not make a trollop out of me!"

Clem began to laugh. Slow and contained at first, his mirth built steadily into an all-out guffaw. Margot flushed a bright red; turning away, she pulled on her robe and picked up her shoes, intent on leaving. Realizing what was happening Clem suddenly stopped laughing and grew very serious.

"Please don't go," Clem said. "There's been a mistake."

"I'll say there has," Margot replied, moving toward the door in a huff.

"I'm not married, and Rhoda is not my wife," Clem said in desperation before Margot could leave the room.

At this, Margot stopped and turned from the door back to Clem.

Clem continued, "Rhoda is the wife of my business partner. Her name is Rhoda Davis. She is journeying with me to assist with the contract and payment issues so I can focus on my jumps. Please, you must believe me. I would never make a fool out of you."

Clem did not want to use the word *trollop* in his response to Margot.

Margot wanted desperately to believe Clem. She turned back to him and looked into his eyes. Clem was looking directly at her. In his eyes, Margot could see that Clem was telling the truth.

"I'm sorry … I feel a little bit silly," Margot said ever so slowly to Clem.

"Please don't feel that way. If you've had this belief, it's partly my fault. I thought I told you in the dining hall, but I must not have," Clem said.

Margot dropped her flats and removed her robe. She walked toward Clem, who was still standing out on the dance floor.

When she was a few feet away, she asked, "Do you know how to help me leap higher, Mister Batman?"

"I think I can help you, Miss Margot," he replied with a grin.

Clem walked over and stood behind Margot. He reached out and held both of her hands. Then, lifting them and outstretching her arms like wings, he whispered into her right ear, "Have you ever felt the sensation of flying?"

"No. Certainly not in the way you have," she answered, a tad breathlessly.

Clem continued, "When I'm in the air, I feel like I'm weightless. I use the air currents to move me here and there. When I look to the horizon, I can see for miles. There is no other feeling like that in the world. Look out beyond the walls of this room. Can you see far, far away?"

"Yes ... I believe I can," Margot replied.

"I know in my heart that someday we will all be able to fly on our own. We'll spread our wings and sail through the sky like eagles. I want to develop the means to make sure that occurs. When you dance, think about this. Put more spring in your legs when you leap, and pretend you're not coming down. Raise your arms with your leap to give you more momentum, and feel the sensation of flying," Clem instructed. Then Clem slowly brought her arms down to her side and let go of Margot's hands.

"Let me start the music and try again," she said.

Margot went back to the record player and pushed the switch to set the turntable in motion. She carefully placed the arm one-half inch from the start of the music and made her way back to Clem.

"Lift me up again when I tell you to," Margot said, "and then let me down slowly."

After a few measures of music were played, Margot said, "Now."

Clem lifted her up full, and gently let her down. She stepped away from him and performed her double-tours. Then moving forward, she began her series of grand jetés. First one, then another, and then another as Margot traveled around the perimeter of the room. She put more strength in her leaps and moved her arms up quickly with each jump. For moments at the peak of her leap, she felt like she was actually flying, and she became overwhelmed with the sensation. She once again landed in front of Clem after completing her steps, then turned and looked into his eyes. This time she reached up as the music continued playing and put her right hand on Clem's cheek. She gently led his mouth to hers and began to give him a deep kiss. Margot had had many opportunities to kiss men at afterglow parties and public events, but she had never felt a kiss like this one with Clem. The music persisted, and Clem and Margot continued to kiss.

"So, you were able to jump higher than before?" I asked.

"I'm certain I have never leapt higher," Margot answered with a wonderful smile on her face that was quite unlike any she had shown up to this point.

I couldn't help but enjoy Margot's expression for a few seconds, but then I felt compelled to ask a question.

"Did you say earlier that Clem believed we would all be able to fly on our own someday?" I asked.

"Clem told me that when he was a young lad in school, he learned about the story of Icarus. Do you know who he is?" Margot asked.

I wanted desperately to say that I did, but nothing was coming to mind. I shook my head.

"No, I don't believe I do. Can you tell me the story?" I asked.

Margot answered, "In Greek mythology, Icarus was the son of a master craftsman working forced-labor on the island of Crete. His father, Daedalus, devised a plan to escape the island by making wings out of bird feathers adhered together with wax. He fashioned the wings and strapped them onto Icarus and himself, then instructed Icarus to follow him closely. Daedalus warned Icarus not to fly too low, avoiding the dampness of the sea that would clog his wings, or too high, avoiding the sun, which would melt the wax. But as Icarus took flight, he was captivated by his own ability to fly, and he disobeyed his father. He flew high above the earth, much too close to the sun. The wax melted his wings and Icarus fell hopelessly to his death, drowning in the sea."

"Now that you tell the story I believe I have heard it before," I admitted to Margot, jotting down a note to read up on the myth later.

"Well, Clem told me that this fable had a lasting impression on him. From the time he heard it, he wanted to fly like Icarus. I suppose this is partially what drove Clem to fulfill his passion as a batman in the sky."

I thought about how I had always viewed learning Greek mythology as a total waste of time. Who could possibly put this information to any use, I'd mused? But I was now learning that what one person sees as folly can be another person's passion.

RACING HEARTS

I thought it wonderful that Clem had been able to help Margot with her dance.

"Did Clem and you get to spend any more time together on the ship?" I asked.

"Yes, quite a bit actually," Margot replied. "We saw each other some part of all of the remaining days of our travel. On April 11, 1937, the last day before we landed in Southampton, England, we spent nearly the entire day together. It was wonderful! It was on that day that I learned so much about Clem and his life. I also got to see his amazing batwings that caused such a sensation."

It was two o'clock in the afternoon, and Clem had just finished lunch with Margot in the Queen Mary's dining hall. The ship was two days late in docking at Southampton due to the weather. Provisions were getting low, and some items on the menu were no longer available. Margot ordered spaghetti milanaise with the sauce on the side from the luncheon menu. She also had a small saucer of barley broth. She was a finicky eater, as she had never acquired a taste for eggs, red meat, or vegetables. Clem had grilled fillets of weakfish with mashed potatoes on the side. He finished his lunch with a slice of blackberry pie. They remained together at the dining table for a while, drinking coffee and conversing.

"Just look at that rain," Clem said as he peered out a small, circular window set above their table. "It's already made us two days late."

"What will you do if it's raining at the French airshow?" Margot asked.

"There will be no jumping in the rain, that's for sure. A parachute needs to be fluffy and completely dry to operate correctly," Clem responded.

"Can you tell me more about what you do? Will you show me your batman suit?" asked Margot.

"I would love to, if it's okay for you to go to my cabin," Clem responded.

"I think that would be fine," Margot said. She felt completely safe with Clem, but there was a slight sense of excitement at the thought of being with him alone in his quarters.

Clem and Margot made their way to Clem's accommodations on the Sun Deck. The rain continued falling monotonously, and the winds from the east persisted. Clem and Margot entered the inner staircase and stayed under the deck awning, keeping out of the rain as they made their way to Clem's cabin. Clem's room was near the ship's stern on the starboard side, eight decks above the After-Engine room. When they reached room S13, Clem pulled his cabin key from the right front pocket of his trousers to unlock the metal door. The door had a round port window four inches in diameter at eye level to let in some natural light. There was another window next to the door on the outside wall, three feet wide by two feet high, which could slide to the side to let in the ocean air. As he turned the key, a familiar voice was heard.

"I see you two have gotten to know each other quite well," said

Mr. Burk, who they had both met in the dining hall days ago. He was taking a walk around the ship holding a rather large glass of bourbon, and spoke with a slight slur.

"Ah … yes we have," Clem responded, feeling a little awkward at what this might have looked like to him.

"Don't worry, Mr. Burk," Margot said. "Clem is just going to take his clothes off and put on his batman suit for me." She winked at Mr. Burk, then turned toward Clem and put her arm in his.

"Hurry, honey, I don't want to miss the excitement!" she continued.

Clem was not prepared for this kind of humor out of Margot, and he immediately blushed with embarrassment.

Mr. Burk got a little wide-eyed before they all broke out in laughter as he continued on his way, swaying slightly.

"I don't think he'll remember this conversation in the morning," Clem said.

"I'm unsure he'll even find his cabin," Margot replied as they both laughed again.

Once inside, Margot found the room to be very tidy and well ordered. This seemed to match the personality of Clem, which she had become accustomed to. His room was eight feet by ten feet in size, and featured one single bed, as well as a small bathroom with a toilet and shower. He had a small six-drawer dresser with which to store his clothing and personal items, and a deck chair. The walls of the cabin were bone white in color, with tan wood trimming the window and doors. Clem had left the window open slightly to air out the room, but it still contained a slight scent of moldiness which the passengers on the ship had become accustomed to after the many days of rain. His parachute and batman outfit were too large for his dresser and were stored beneath his bed in canvas bags. After they entered his room, Clem immediately opened the curtain and slid the window to one-half open to let in more ocean air.

"Please sit down, Margot," Clem said as he motioned toward the deck chair.

Margot sat in the chair. She removed a brown, wool bowler hat adorned with cock pheasant feathers from her head and set it on the floor next to her chair.

"Oh, please let me take that," Clem stated as he picked her hat up from the floor and placed it on his dresser.

"Would you like a glass of water?" he continued.

"Yes, I would like that," Margot replied.

Clem filled a glass cup with a Cunard-White Star Line logo from a small pitcher on his dresser and handed it to Margot. Margot gripped the glass, took a sip, and then held it in her hands on her lap.

"Your room is quite nice," Margot said. "Much nicer than the tourist class accommodations I am staying in."

"I didn't ask for this cabin. I would have been fine with third class, but the captain insisted that I stay in one of the best cabins on the ship. It's an advantage of being a celebrity, I guess," Clem responded. As he spoke, he realized that Margot was also a celebrity, and he wished inside that she had received this special treatment instead of him.

"Well, it is wonderful, and I'm glad they gave it to you," Margot said.

Clem sat on the side of his bed facing Margot. He looked into her eyes and was lost for words. Margot, too, was caught up in this wonderful moment together and sat looking at Clem. The silence started to make them both feel a little uneasy.

"Where do you keep your flight gear?" Margot asked, breaking the silence.

"It's under my bed. There's really no other place to store it. Here, I'll show you," Clem replied.

Clem got down on his knees and pulled one of the canvas bags out from below his bed.

"This is where I keep my flight suit," Clem said. "The other bag contains my parachutes."

Clem lifted the bag and placed it on his bed. There was a noticeable damp spot on the bottom of the bag, and Clem brushed at the spot with his hand. Having made no impression on the damp area, Clem positioned the bag so that the spot was on top and not touching the bed. He unsnapped the buckle on top of the bag and opened it. Reaching into the bag, he pulled out a shiny, white overall. It was compressed and wrinkled due to the many days in the unopened bag. Clem grabbed the shoulder portion and shook it a few times to try and remove the crinkles. He opened it up and laid it out on the bed, with the shoulders at the head of the bed and the legs toward its foot. Clem then spread out the wrinkled material to show the fabric sewn in between the legs, and the straps protruding from the bottom of his pant legs to keep them secured at the arches of his feet. All of the fabric was zephyr cloth, which was a heavy fabric used for sales on boats. The zephyr cloth replaced the cotton canvas cloth he'd started out with three years earlier. Margot got up from the chair and set her water glass on Clem's dresser. She went over to the bed and put her hand on the right arm of the flight suit.

"My, this is amazing," Margot said. "How ever did you have this made?"

Clem replied, "The flight suit is a military issue. The cloth between the legs I attached myself using my mother's sewing machine."

"She must be a strong lady to let you do something so daring," Margot noted as she felt the material of his outfit.

"It's actually my step-mother's sewing machine," Clem observed. "My real mom passed when I was a small child. She did all of her stitching by hand. I don't know what my mom would have thought about me doing what I do ... but I somehow think she would approve." As he spoke, Clem conjured up a memory of his mom hand-sewing an American Indian Halloween costume that he'd worn as a child.

"I'm so sorry, Clem," Margot said remorsefully.

"Please don't feel bad, Margot. I loved my mother and still do. She is in a good place," Clem explained. "Now, what do you think about me as a seamstress?" He said this with a smile on his face, clearly trying to change the subject.

"I think you did a wonderful job. Do you make women's apparel as well?" Margot replied with a twinkle in her eye.

Clem began to laugh as he said, "Yes, as a matter of fact. I make costumes for the U.S. Air Force ballet." Margot found his reply very amusing and laughed a bit.

"What is this for?" Margot asked as she touched a weighted piece of cloth sewn in the middle of the added material.

"The material stitched between my legs is used as a horizontal stabilizer, like the tail of a bird or the back wings of a plane. This weighted piece helps me keep my legs plumb as I drop down from the sky," Clem explained.

"Is it cumbersome to wear?" Margot asked.

"It's burdensome to walk in and ugly as sin, but in the air, it makes the descent much more stable," Clem replied.

"Do you have your wings here as well?" Margot asked.

"Oh yes, I do," Clem answered.

He set the flight suit aside to make room for another part of his outfit. He then reached into the canvas bag and pulled out the wing portion. This was rather heavy. It was a metal pipe cage that wrapped around the back of his torso and was strapped at his chest, waist, and over his shoulders. The wings were attached on each side of this pipe cage. The innermost part of the wing fabric was sewn around a pipe for the full length of the three-foot cage that straddled Clem's torso. The rest of the cloth wing covered four ribs of metal, which all hinged at the top of the pipe frame. The very top ribs had small, wooden paddles that Clem could hold in his hands to extend or retract the wings. There was a zipper along the full length of the middle of each wing, which allowed for the wings to be opened if the ribs or frame needed attention or examination. At the tip of each rib was a piece of leather sewn into the material to keep the rib frame from poking through the zephyr cloth. The wings were showing much wear and were dirty and dull, in stark contrast to the flight suit. There were little tears and worn spots throughout the wings, and minor repairs with shoestrings where strong nylon rope once held. Clem laid the retracted wings mechanism on the bed for Margot to view and then spread the left side to reveal a fully extended wing.

This did not seem at all safe to Margot. While she was impressed with the engineering that went into the design and fabrication of the wing apparatus, she was surprised at how beaten and worn it was.

"Did you make this, too?" Margot asked.

"Yes, I did, every part of it," Clem responded with great pride.

"It looks like it's time for you to make yourself a new set of wings," Margot commented.

"These wings will do fine for me for now," Clem replied.

"Our wardrobe mistress, Mrs. Newman, is a wonderful seamstress … almost as good as you," Margot said with a smile. "If you showed this to her, I'm sure she could sew you wings from new material, which would look wonderful."

"These will do just fine," Clem repeated. After this comment, there was a brief, awkward silence. Finally, Clem asked, "Can you keep a secret for me, Margot?"

"Why certainly, Clem," she responded.

"I am quitting after this airshow," Clem said. "I won't be needing these wings in a few weeks."

"You're quitting?" Margot asked, somewhat in disbelief.

"Margot, have you ever felt so scared of dying that you have seen your life flash before your eyes? Well, I have. I made light of the accident in England last year, but in the last few feet I truly thought I was going to die. The truth is that if I hadn't landed on the top of a car, I would have." Clem stepped toward the window and looked out at the rain pouring down hard and steady on the ocean waves.

Clem continued, "I've seen friends of mine, good friends, die at airshows performing jumps and flights to please the crowds. I've heard of others trying to copy my feats that have gone into death spins, lost consciousness, and died. I want to end this all before it happens to me."

Margot made her way beside Clem and took his hand. Clem turned and looked into her eyes. After this brief exchange, Clem and Margot embraced. After a few seconds, they released from their tight hold and then began to kiss. As they kissed, their minds flew to incredible heights and their hearts raced: For both of them, this kiss was like no other. There was so much passion and desire in their souls for each other.

Clem smelled the wonderful scent of Margot as he moved his mouth from one side to the other. It was the breathtaking fragrance of a woman. In his adult years, he had met women who interested him, but none that he felt he truly loved. Margot was different. Everything about her was exciting and wonderful. She was someone he felt he could love forever, and he did not want to ever leave her impassioned embrace.

Margot for her part felt the hard muscles of Clem. Although amazing and strong men had held her during performances, none felt quite like Clem did. His rugged good looks and inquisitive smile caused her to stir like she had never been stirred in the past. She held him ever so closely and tightly. She also felt this was an experience that she did not want to end. But soon the embrace was relaxed, and Clem and Margot backed away slightly from each other to glimpse into each other's eyes.

"Promise me you'll be careful in France," Margot requested.

"I will … just for you," Clem responded.

"Clem and I really found peace and happiness on that evening," Margot said to Ren as she wiped a small tear from the corner of her eye.

"Do you think that this was love at first sight?" I asked.

"In the rest of my life I have never felt so moved by a man," Margot answered. "I'm not sure that I can describe true love for your story, but I know I felt it."

"What else did you talk about?" I asked.

"An easier answer is what didn't we talk about? We spent the better part of the day and on into the evening sharing about our lives. That is how I learned so much about Clem. We probably would have talked all night had we not gotten interrupted," Margot explained.

SCANDAL

"**Y**ou were interrupted?" I asked.

"Have you ever been so involved in something that you totally lost track of time?" Margot asked.

"Sure," I responded.

"Well, that's what happened to Clem and me," Margot continued. "Clem told me all about his life, and I told him about mine. We laughed, and we cried. We held each other and we kissed. It was an amazing and wonderful evening. But time got away from us, and we totally lost track. This caused a stir with my dance troupe."

At 11:30 p.m. that evening, the rain began to let up. Clem and Margot were still enjoying each other's marathon conversation in Clem's cabin. Hours earlier, Clem had turned on his cabin lights as the daylight diminished. There was no clock visible in Clem's room, and neither Margot nor Clem carried a timepiece. Their discussion was so new and interesting that there was no thought of time at all between them. They were finding out that they loved each other, and time holds no boundaries on love.

It was not unusual for Margot to be out and about on the ship, but it was unusual for her to not be in her room by 8 p.m. Gwyneth had lain down shortly after 8 p.m. and had fallen asleep. But when she woke at 11:30 and found Margot's bed still empty, she became alarmed. Not knowing what to do, she put on her robe and walked outside to Frederick Ashton's cabin. She rapped on his door.

"Frederick … are you awake?" she asked somewhat quietly, so as not to disturb other travelers who might be sleeping.

When no response was returned after a reasonable amount of time, she repeated her action with a slightly elevated volume. At this, Gwyneth could hear Frederick stir. In a few seconds, the door opened slightly.

"Who is calling and what is it you want?" Frederick asked.

"It's Gwyneth, and I don't know where Margot is," was her reply.

"When was the last time you saw her?" Frederick questioned.

"She left our room before noon. I think she was going to lunch."

"Do you have any idea where she might be?"

Gwyneth answered, "I guess she could be at the music room, but she doesn't generally stay out this late."

"I'll go there with you in a second and see if we can find her," Frederick suggested.

Frederick put on some casual clothes and a pair of deck shoes before meeting Gwyneth outside of his cabin. Together they walked to the music room and found it empty.

"Do you have any other ideas as to where she might be?" Frederick asked.

"She has been spending a lot of time with Clem Sohn. She might be with him somewhere," Gwyneth replied.

"Let's go to a concierge and find out where Clem is staying," Frederick replied, his calm tone giving no intimation of his misgivings.

On each deck of the ship was an information counter. These areas were staffed to assist passengers with questions about the ship and the amenities within. After seven days on the ship, most passengers were well-acclimated to everything about the ship, and there was little need for information dispersion at this point. Frederick and Gwyneth went straight to the information counter and found a young assistant fast asleep in a deck chair behind it.

"Sir, sir … " Frederick sounded while hitting the desk bell, "can you help us locate a passenger?"

The young gentleman had blond hair and was dressed in a bright red blazer and black pants. He jumped out of his seat and quickly stood behind the counter. A name tag on his lapel read *William*.

"Yes, how can I help you?"

"We are looking for a passenger … a Margot Fonteyn. She has not returned to her room tonight, and we're a little worried about her," Frederick said.

"I can call the ship's security team if you'd like," replied William.

"I think that is a good idea," Frederick responded, looking at Gwyneth. She nodded her head in agreement.

"Okay, please fill out this request form for me while I contact them," William responded.

He pulled a tablet from below the counter and handed it to Frederick. Frederick took the tablet and immediately gave it to Gwyneth to write out the details of the request.

"I would also like to know where a Clem Sohn is staying, if you don't mind," Frederick continued.

"Is this connected to the missing passenger?" William asked.

"We're not sure," replied Frederick, "but they have been spending a good deal of time together in the last few days."

William pulled out a ledger book from under the counter and opened it up. He turned it around for Frederick to view and then picked up a telephone handset.

"Operator, can you please connect me to the security team?" William asked.

The ledger book was neatly handwritten with the names, ages, occupations, and assigned cabin numbers for each of the 1,987 passengers on the ship. The book was in alphabetical order by last name, and Frederick quickly turned to the pages with names that started with the letter "S."

"Hello, security team?" William requested. "I've received notification of a missing passenger."

After a brief pause, William held his hand over the receiver and asked Frederick, "What was the name of the passenger again?"

"Margot Fonteyn," Frederick responded, somewhat annoyed.

"Yes, Margot Fonteyn," William replied to the person on the other end of the line. "I suggest you locate the cabin of a Clem Song and start there."

"That's Sohn, NOT SONG," Frederick said in an elevated tone, "and he's in cabin S-13, according to the passenger log."

"Sorry, that's Clem Sohn in cabin S-13," William relayed to the security team. "Okay, I'll wait for your call."

"I'm going there, too; where is this cabin located?" Frederick asked.

"S-13 is several flights up and to the back of the ship," William responded. "The security team has an office location near there and will be at the cabin before you even get to the stairway. Please relax until we can have that checked out."

Gwyneth had finished filling out the request form by this time and slid the tablet to William. He looked it over and said, "Can you please both sign this on the dotted lines at the bottom?"

William handed the tablet back to Frederick and Gwyneth for their signatures. As they signed the form, Fritz, an officer of the Queen Mary security team, was making his way toward Clem's cabin. He was dressed as an English constable in a dark suit with a black helmet and a nightstick supported by his belt. As he neared, he could see lights on in the cabin. He peered into the window, now nearly completely closed due to the chilly night air. Upon looking inside, Fritz saw Margot sitting on a chair smiling and laughing at something Clem had just said, while Clem was sitting on the bed looking at Margot with an equally large smile. Fritz rapped on the door. Clem got up and opened the door a small amount and asked, "Can I help you?"

"Yes, are you Clem Sohn?" Fritz asked.

"Yes, I am, is there a problem?" Clem responded.

"I'm here in response to a missing passenger request."

"I can assure you that I am not missing," Clem confidently replied.

"The request wasn't for you. It was for a Margot Fonteyn," Fritz explained. He glanced beyond Clem into the cabin, hand falling casually to his nightstick.

"That's me," Margot said as Clem opened the door wider so that the security officer could see who had responded.

"Is everything okay here, ma'am?" Fritz persisted.

"Yes, of course," Margot replied. She started blushing.

"Would it be okay if I escorted you back to your cabin for the evening?" Fritz asked, relaxing his stance somewhat.

"Please, let me do that," Clem insisted.

"Oh? Can I trust that you will get her there in a timely fashion?"

"Most assuredly," Clem responded. "We'll leave right now."

Fritz left and went back to the security desk to call William and apprise him of the situation. When William received the call, he let Frederick and Gwyneth know that Margot had been found, and that she was returning to her cabin with Clem.

"That must have been a little embarrassing," I noted.

"Not really," Margot replied. "I cherished the time I spent with Clem and would not change a single thing. I knew I was in love with him that day."

"Did you get into trouble with the dance troupe over this?" I asked.

"Ha, no. You have to remember that we had spent a week on the ship in continually stormy weather going across the Atlantic. We were all about to dock in Southampton the next day, and that was the most prominent event on everyone's mind."

LONELY MAN

"What did you do next?" I asked Margot.

"Our journey across the Atlantic finally ended the next day," Margot replied. "Because of the continual rain experienced during the trip across the ocean, we were all so very tired and anxious to step foot on dry land. That morning the weather was calm, clear, and sunny for the first time on the trip, and everyone was in high spirits. The windows and doors of the many cabins and rooms on the ship were opened wide to let in the cool, clean air, while letting out the musty smells that had accumulated from the many days of rain. I had mixed feelings about the day, because the ocean crossing had been such a wonderful journey with Clem. I was anxious to get home, but wondered how this change of venue would affect Clem and me."

On the late morning of Monday, April 12, 1937, the Queen Mary made its way into the English Channel and up the East Cowes Waterway to finally dock in Southampton Port. The weather had caused the ship's schedule from New York to be delayed two days. This meant that the subsequent trip to Cherbourg, France, was also delayed until April 19, the following Monday. The ship would remain berthed in Southampton in order to be cleaned and restocked with provisions for the trips to France and back to the United States.

The highest priority for the ship's crew was to disembark the large number of passengers whose final destination was England. Other passengers were asked to remain on the vessel until this activity was completed. Margot and her dance troupe were departing in England, while Clem and Rhoda would take the ship on to Cherbourg. Clem went down to Margot and Gwyneth's second-class cabin and assisted them by carrying their luggage to the gangplank. He brought with him Margot's brown bowler hat, which had been left in his cabin the evening before. He awkwardly handed it to Margot in the presence of Gwyneth, a stark reminder of the previous evening's scandalous commotion.

The British Ballet dance troupe had received preferential treatment for disembarking the ship, and they left together as one group near the front of the line. Clem and Margot spoke before Margot stepped off the ship, and they made plans to see each other during his brief stay in England. She gave Clem directions to the Sadler's Wells Theatre in London, and times when she would be there practicing for her dance numbers in the *Les Patineurs* and *Carnival* productions.

Clem stood at the ship's rail as Margot and the rest of her dance troupe left the ship. As she walked away on the port dock, she turned to look back at Clem and blew a kiss to him. Clem's heart ached for Margot, and this simple gesture made him desire her more than ever. It seemed like a part of him was leaving when he saw her walk slowly away.

There were so many passengers to account for, and so much paperwork to reconcile, that the off-boarding took the rest of the day to complete. At around 7 p.m., the last of the disembarking took place, and an impatient Clem (accompanied by Rhoda) left the ship to take in the sights of Southampton. Gas streetlights adorned the thoroughfares of the town and provided safe passage along the sidewalks. There was much gratitude in the hearts of Clem and Rhoda for finally being on land. They intended to walk for a long distance before going back to the ship for the night.

From the port, they walked north four kilometers to the Star Hotel. A menu behind a window of the building along the sidewalk reminded them that they should consider eating dinner. They went inside and sat in the pub area. Clem thought it was nice to go somewhere where patrons didn't know who he was. He sincerely loved the attention he sometimes received for being a batman, but on this night, he was feeling a little forlorn. He was missing Margot and wanted to be left to his thoughts. They sat down at a table by a window and each drank ale while eating a meal of roast beef with garden beans and Yorkshire pudding.

"Is there anything you need before we leave for France next week?" Rhoda asked.

Clem was deep in thought about Margot. He was looking at his unfinished plate of food and twisting his draft of ale with his right hand.

"Clem … is there anything you need before we leave for France?" Rhoda repeated, with increased volume.

Clem blinked and looked up from his half-eaten meal. "I'm sorry," he responded, realizing she had spoken to him earlier. "I don't think so."

Another twenty seconds went by without conversation as Rhoda watched Clem twist his glass.

"You really miss her, don't you?" Rhoda inquired.

Clem blinked again, then smiled softly. "Yes, I do. I've never met anyone like her. She has a powerful spirit, like I remember my mother having. I plan to see her again before we leave for France."

"I'm sure that we can make that happen. We have a few days to kill here, after all," Rhoda acknowledged. "But … what will you do when we have to go back to the United States?"

"I don't know," Clem replied. "I told Margot that I want to quit jumping. Maybe I can stay in England for a while, see how English living suits me."

"What about your commitments back home?" Rhoda wondered.

"I don't know, Rhoda … I just don't know," Clem replied. He returned to his thoughts of Margot.

"You've told me before—I don't know how many times—that you want to quit jumping. But then you get to an airshow and see the crowds and hear their applause … when that happens, it seems like you want to jump again all the more," Rhoda noted.

"Yes, that's true. But I've never felt like this before. I've needed the applause and the admiration in the past because I've had no one … no one to love," Clem replied. "I may be a tough reckless character in a crowd, but deep inside, I'm just a lonely man, Rhoda. A pathetic and very lonely man." Clem began to shed tears as he continued, "I don't want to go forward being as I am. I want something different … something more. I have more money than I know what to do with, yet I still live at home with my dad. I'm twenty-six years old! What kind of life is that?" He bowed his head, shoulders shaking silently. "Maybe it's finally time for Icarus to return to earth. Before his wings melt."

"Oh, Clem, don't be so hard on yourself," Rhoda advised. "Let's get through this airshow first, and we can talk about the future later. Did you repack your parachute?"

"No," Clem replied, wiping at his already-drying cheeks. "There's lots of time for that. I'd like to find out how I can get a ride to London tomorrow. I'll ask at the concierge desk."

Clem got up and went to speak with the hotel concierge. Rhoda sat at the table waiting for Clem's return.

When Clem came back to the table, he put down enough British-pound coins to cover the meal, generous tip included. Then he and Rhoda made their way back to the ship for the night.

"Poor Clem," I said. "He must have been heartbroken."

Margot replied, "Yes, he was. He told me about this conversation the next day when he came to London to see me. While Clem was feeling heartbroken in Southampton, I was having my own personal pity party on the way to London."

The dance troupe took a train to London. Margot sat in a window seat, appearing to stare silently at the passing landscape. In actuality, she was dwelling on Clem and the conversations they had shared over the last week. Elizabeth Miller, who was called Betsy by the troupe, sat down next to her and struck up a conversation.

"Are you glad to be back home in England?" Betsy asked.

"Yes, I truly am," Margot replied. After a brief silence, she continued, "Can you keep a secret?"

"Of course, I can," Betsy replied. "Is it about Clem?"

"Why, yes. However, did you know?"

"You didn't exactly make it a secret that you were spending time with him. When you were out late with him on Sunday night, it made for some tantalizing gossip," Betsy explained.

"I guess it was a little scandalous, wasn't it?" Margot agreed with a smirk on her face. "I've fallen in love with Clem. He has a spirit that I cannot resist. Clem is gentle, thoughtful, and very kind ... but also brave. He's exactly what I imagined I'd find in a man I could marry. Moreover, he's a genuine dreamer—he actually thinks that he can design a suit that will let people fly like birds."

"What will you do when he has to go back to the States?" Betsy asked.

"I don't know … I just don't know," Margot replied. "I hope that Clem and I can work out some kind of plan before he leaves. We didn't speak about this before I left the ship."

Betsy responded, "I'm a little jealous of you. Clem is dashing, and seeing the gracious way he handled the attention he received from the ship's crew and passengers has made me wonder what it would be like to have such a wonderful man."

Margot seemed to drift off into a private world in her mind. It was a place she had filled with personal thoughts, beyond expression. I couldn't help but ask an obvious question.

"Did you get to make a plan with Clem about your futures?" I asked.

"Sort of," Margot replied. "Clem came to London the very next day with Rhoda, and we were able to spend some time together, talking about the next phase of our relationship."

Through the Star Hotel concierge, Clem learned about the rail system between Southampton and London. The next morning, he purchased tickets at the Southampton Central Train Station for Rhoda and himself to make the trip. They arrived in London at 9:45 a.m., at the Waterloo station. From there they took three rail connections to finally arrive in the Clerkenwell district of London (where the Sadler's Wells Theatre was located) at 11 a.m.

They went to the theater's front door, facing on Rosebery Avenue, and entered. The theater had a rich historical tradition. Originally opening in 1683, the building had gone through several renovations. The last round of major renovations had been completed just six years earlier, in 1931, and the building was grand indeed. Once inside, they could immediately hear the sound of orchestra music in a distant room. As they made their way through the lobby toward the sound, Clem recognized it as the music Margot had played in the ship's music hall when they'd danced together. It was an opportune time to be there, for when they pulled back the curtain to the audience entrance of the auditorium there was Margot onstage performing the pas di deux from the *Les Patineurs* production with Robert Helpmann. Clem and Rhoda were immediately mesmerized by Margot's dancing. She looked absolutely angelic as she bounded gracefully across the stage. This was the first time Rhoda had seen Margot dance, and it gave her a new perspective on her. Up to now, Margot had appeared to her to be frail and without passion. Seeing her powerful body and the preciseness of her dance made Rhoda realize that Margot was in fact an expert at her craft, a highly trained and impassioned professional.

As the dance continued Clem and Rhoda both developed tears in their eyes from the sheer beauty of the ballet number. Margot was so intensely focused on her part that she did not see or know that guests were watching. When she began her series of grand jetés, Clem remembered her struggles with her lifts and the advice he had given her. She appeared to be much improved from Clem's memory of her earlier efforts, and he was immensely proud of her. When this part of the dance was completed and the music stopped, the dance troupe (who were seated in the first few rows of the auditorium) erupted in applause. To this, Margot and Robert gave a long stage bow to their peer admirers.

After the applause subsided and the phonograph stopped playing, Margot looked into the audience area and saw Clem and Rhoda walking down the aisle toward the stage. Margot could not contain herself and ran excitedly offstage, winding through a maze of curtains to arrive down in the auditorium area. She ran to Clem and put her arms around him and then around Rhoda.

"I'm so happy to see you," Margot said, with obvious excitement in her voice.

"I'm so very happy to see you, too," Clem answered, reaching out to hold her again. He did not want to let go. He picked her up and swung her around in a circle before easing her down to the floor.

"I think we're finished with your numbers today, Margot," Frederick Ashton said from the front center row of seats. "Please enjoy your guests."

With that, Margot grabbed Clem's left hand with her right and said, "Please follow me, you two."

Margot took them through some winding hallways to her dressing room behind the stage area. She opened the door and asked them to both come in. Her dressing room was a four-foot by six-foot room with a two-foot by three-foot mirror affixed on the long wall. Along each side of the mirror were many pictures of various sizes stuck between the mirror and the wall by their corners. Below the mirror was a wooden makeup credenza with three drawers across the top, an open area in the middle below the drawers, and small cabinet doors on each side below the drawers. On the top of the credenza was a white wooden makeup box with extension trays on each side and a mirror on the top that doubled as the lid when the box was closed. Next to the makeup box on top of the credenza were all sorts of makeup products scattered about. Some of the makeup products were laying there open, as if Margot had hastily left the room for her performance sans time to tidy things up. It was certainly a picture of disarray, not unlike what might be found in someone's personal area when not expecting visitors. There was a small wooden chair in front of the credenza, which Margot sat on to begin freshening up. Clem was certainly out of his element in this room, and the smells and sights were absolutely foreign to him. He was, however, excited to see Margot in this little refuge of hers, which few other people were ever able to see. Margot grabbed a white towel and dipped it into a De Belleza Robert cold cream container and began to use the mixture to take off the makeup she had applied earlier.

"We can leave for a spell if you'd like," Clem said, feeling a bit uneasy in these surroundings.

"Yes, let's go and give Margot some privacy so she can freshen up," Rhoda agreed.

"Nonsense," Margot said, "just give me a second and I'll be ready." As she spoke she looked at Clem through the reflection in her mirror. Clem was looking intently at her. Their eyes met: Clem thought she looked incredibly beautiful as she wiped the towel on her smooth skin. He wanted to say so, but refrained in Rhoda's presence.

"I told Mum all about you two, and she is anxious to meet you," Margot said. "I hope you can come by our house and join us for tea and cake."

"I can think of nothing I'd rather do," Clem replied.

Rhoda nodded in agreement. Within minutes, Margot finished removing her makeup. She then backed the chair away from the credenza and took off her ballet slippers. She opened a cabinet door below her credenza and slid her baffies inside, pulling out a pair of flats before closing the door. After this, she grabbed a red and black plaid skirt that had been hanging on a hall tree in the corner behind her chair. She stepped inside the skirt and hiked it up over her off-white leotard to her waist before tying the waist strings. She then took a black overcoat from the same hall tree and put it on. Once she was properly dressed, she stopped for a second to look around and determine if she was ready to leave.

"I think that's everything," she said. "Let's be on our way."

Margot, Rhoda, and Clem left the theater and took a public

transport to Margot's home. Clem and Rhoda were relieved to be riding with someone who knew London's labyrinthine public transportation system.

"I can only imagine how Clem must have felt, being in your dressing room for the first time," I commented to Margot with a sideways smile.

Margot chuckled and winked. "I'm sure he was uneasy, but I simply could not let him out of my sight. I missed him ever so much the night before ... I held my pillow in my arms and dreamt it was him until I finally fell asleep."

PRETTY BOY

"What did your mom think of Clem?" I asked.

Margot replied, "Clem was so nervous when he arrived at my house. It caused him to create quite a spectacle. Mum liked him well enough … eventually. He was so polite and kind, quite unlike most of the men I kept company with in the dance profession. In some ways, Clem seemed bashful and quiet, which struck me as a little strange given the following he had all over the world. I guess Clem never dwelled on how much of a hero he actually was. He had a sincere heart and just wanted to entertain and please people."

Margot, Rhoda, and Clem disembarked from the Piccadilly Line at Russell Square and walked nearly one kilometer to 47 Lamb Conduit Street, where Margot lived with her mother. They arrived there very close to noontime. Margot opened the front door at street level and entered. She stepped inside, turned to her guests, and said, "Please come in."

Clem and Rhoda followed up a flight of stairs and then another to apartment 3B. Margot opened the door without a key and announced their arrival.

"Mum, I'm here with Clem and Rhoda," Margot said in a loud voice.

"You're early, Peg," came a response from a woman in a distant room. "I wasn't expecting any guests, but I'll put on some tea for all of you. Your brother Felix is here. Go ahead and sit in the parlor, and I'll bring you some refreshments."

"Did your mother call you Peg?" Rhoda asked as they made their way down a short hallway to the parlor.

"Yes," replied Margot. "Margot Fonteyn is my stage name. My real name is Margaret Hookham. Mum started calling me Peg after one of my early dance teachers gave me that nickname. I was about twelve years old at the time. I don't mind; I like the name Peg."

They took a few steps farther, encountering a threshold on the left leading into an open sitting area where Margot's brother Felix was already settled. The sitting room was fourteen-feet square and painted in a neutral cream color. It had two three-feet wide by four-feet tall windows facing the street on the east wall, which were each comprised of four large panes accented with white lace curtains. The windows could be opened to let in the outside air when needed, but they stood closed on this cool spring day. There was a three-cushion sofa along the south wall, and two wood-framed cushion chairs were placed along the west wall. There was a small smoking table between the two chairs, with no visible evidence of a smoker living inside. On the north wall there was a large, stately birdcage with a beautiful sulfur-crested cockatoo sitting quietly on a perch inside, and another cushion chair matching the two along the west wall. The room had a dark, wooden floor with a beautiful eight-foot diameter woolen carpet in the center. The carpet had a French design, which included an eight-inch border pattern of single flowers. The room was clean and welcoming, but there was a hint of cat dander in the air. When Rhoda and Clem entered the room behind Margot, Felix stood up and walked up to greet them.

"Greetings, I'm Felix," he said with a grin, holding out his hand to Rhoda, who entered ahead of Clem.

"Hello, I'm Rhoda," Rhoda responded, shaking his hand.

"And I'm Clem Sohn," Clem added as he stepped forward.

"I know all about you," Felix said, giving Clem a firm handshake. "I've been reading about you in the *Times*. Tell me, what was it like to come so close to death in London last year?"

This was something that Clem was often asked, but he never liked answering. To answer meant that he relived the experience to some extent, and that was definitely not something he enjoyed. He had developed a pat answer to it over time, which he gave to satisfy Felix.

"It was the scariest moment in my life. I hope I never go through that again," Clem replied. "I had a split second to make the right move. If I would have waited half a second more, I probably wouldn't be standing here talking to you."

When Clem said this, it really touched Margot. She suddenly felt a strange misgiving about the French airshow and wished in her heart that he wasn't going there.

Felix had been sitting on the sofa but moved to one of the cushioned chairs on the west wall. Margot motioned for Clem to sit on the end of the sofa, to which he obliged. Margot sat in the middle cushion of the sofa, while Rhoda sat next to her on the other end.

Hilda entered the room with a tray of tea and pikelets sprinkled lightly with sugar. The tea service consisted of five teacups and a matching teapot that were all red-clay colored, a distinct matching Asian symbol affixed to each. There was also a cup filled with sugar cubes and a small creamer in the shape of a brown cow, with the tail as a handle and the spout being the cow's mouth. The tea service was a gift that Margot's father had given her mother when they lived in Shanghai. Hilda set the tray down on a coffee table located near the center of the room in front of the sofa and began confidently pouring tea for everyone, starting with Rhoda and Clem. After she finished distributing the tea, she handed the plate of pikelets to Clem, indicating with a nod that he should offer some to Margot and Rhoda. She then sat down on a chair next to Felix and started up a conversation.

"Welcome! I'm Hilda, and I'm so very glad to meet both of you. Peg has told me much about you in the short time since she arrived back home."

"All of it good, I hope?" Clem questioned as he placed the plate of pikelets back on the serving tray.

"Oh yes. If there's one thing Peg truly loves, it's people. I don't know if I've ever heard her say a sour word about anyone," Hilda noted.

"We have certainly enjoyed Margot's company and the company of the dance troupe during our journey on the Queen Mary," Rhoda commented.

"Didn't you grow tired of their shop-talk?" Felix asked. "It seems like they speak an entirely different language when they get together."

"I for one never felt …" Clem began.

Suddenly, as he was speaking, a cat (which had been hunched on the floor next to the sofa, undetected to this point) jumped up onto the arm next to Clem. This startled Clem, and he quickly raised both of his arms and legs into the air, sending his nearly full teacup and saucer flying. The raising of his legs bumped the coffee table, tipping it over, and spilling its contents onto the carpet. Clem stood up quickly and tried to grab the disrupted objects, hoping to minimize the damage; leaning forward just a little too much, he began to lose his balance. Unable to step forward because of the overturned coffee table, Clem slowly fell face-first onto the floor with a loud "Oof!"

In shock at the disaster that had just befallen Clem, everyone in the room (including Clem) remained motionless for a few seconds. The contents of the table were strewn over the floor: Clem was lying in a puddled amalgamation of sugar, pikelets, and spilled tea. Clem slowly turned his head and looked toward Hilda, who was giving him a stern look of concern. As if to show that its diabolic plan had been executed to perfection, the cat jumped from the sofa's arm onto the middle of Clem's back and settled into a sitting position. Just then, the cockatoo spoke up shrilly: "Pretty Boy, Pretty Boy, raaaawk!"

At this, everyone burst into laughter.

"Can I guess the name of the cat?" Clem grunted, still lying on the floor.

"Pretty Boy!" Felix exclaimed between bouts of laughter.

Fortunately, none of the tea service items were broken. All that was damaged was the tea-stained carpet and Clem's pride.

"Poor Clem must have felt terrible," I said to Margot while laughing a little to myself.

Margot replied, "Oh yes! He wanted to be the perfect gentleman to impress my mum, but everything started out so terribly wrong. Clem slowly got up from the floor and helped clean everything up. He eventually took us all out to lunch as well. By the end of the evening, he was Mum's best friend."

"Did you see Clem more during his time in England?" I asked.

"Yes, I did," Margot replied. "I was fortunate enough to see him three of the last five days he was in Southampton. I was able to acquire an automobile from Richard Ellis, who was one of the dancers in our troupe. With his car we took a trip to Devon on the first day, walking the beaches and seeing the sites. On the second day, we drove north through the English countryside to Newcastle, where we walked the town and spent time at Durham Cathedral. That was a day I will never forget. It was then that Clem exposed his true feelings for me, and I for him."

After arriving back at Margot's home, Clem and Margot decided to go for a walk. They headed north, arriving soon at the park in Mecklenburgh Square. It was early spring, but the daffodils along the sidewalk had bloomed, announcing the certainty of warm weather just around time's corner.

"The daffodils look lovely, don't they?" Clem asked.

"They do," replied Margot.

"Like you …" continued Clem, and sighed. "I have had a most wonderful couple of days with you in England."

"I have loved my time with you as well," Margot replied, a slight flutter in her voice.

They stopped and turned to look into each other's eyes. Clem leaned forward and embraced Margot, and kissed her on her waiting lips. They held each other in a deep clasp for several seconds. Finally, their lips parted, but not for want of either one of them.

"I have a problem," Clem finally stated after a few long, breathless seconds.

"What's that?" Margot asked, backing away slightly in concern.

"I can't let go of you," Clem admitted. A broad grin lit up his face.

"That doesn't seem like a problem at all," Margot returned. "I have the same feelings."

"So, what do we do about this?" Clem asked.

Margot gently removed herself from Clem's embrace and took his hand. They began to walk silently toward a nearby swing set.

When they arrived in silence, Margot released Clem's hand and sat on one of the swings.

"Can you give me a little push?" Margot asked.

"Of course, honey," Clem replied.

He moved behind her and gave her a push. As she began to move back and forth, he continued to push her, causing her to rise ever-higher. When she finally achieved a substantial height, Clem sat on the swing next to her and began to swing himself. Soon the two of them were swinging next to each other at the same swooping height. Margot began to laugh.

"We're flying!" she exclaimed.

"Isn't it wonderful?" Clem responded.

They continued to swing in silence for several minutes until Margot began letting her swings diminish. Clem followed in kind, and soon they were stopped and sitting on their respective swings.

"So, do you suppose that is why we love each other?" Margot asked. "We both relish the feeling of floating in the air?"

Clem got off of his swing and moved to stand in front of Margot.

"I suppose that is one thing we have in common, but it's not why I love you," Clem responded. "I have never felt the way I feel in your presence. You are everything to me. I love the very breath you breathe, the ground you walk on, and your touch ..." He shivered. "When we are old and have lost our agility, I will love you even more than I do today."

Margot stood up and reached out to hold Clem.

"I love you, too, ever so much. I don't care what happens in the future, I only know that I love you and need you. I will be yours forever," she promised.

They embraced once again, holding each other for several minutes. There was never so much love felt by either one of them, before or in times to come. They clung to each other and fantasized about a wonderful future spent together—about growing old with each other.

I could tell by Margot's words and her tone of voice that she had returned to that very moment in time as she spoke of it. How wonderful it must have been, I thought, to be so deeply in love! I had never experienced that kind of love before and wondered if I ever would. Looking over my notes, I saw that Margot had mentioned three final days with Clem but had only mentioned two so far.

"What did you do on your third day with Clem?" I asked.

"The last time I saw him was on Sunday, April 18th. He was in the audience to view our production of *Les Patineurs*. The house was full that evening, and there was so much energy in the building. I knew about where Clem and Rhoda were sitting in the audience, but they were too far back for me to make eye contact with them. This was the only time Rhoda and Clem saw me perform in my professional capacity."

"How did you dance that night?"

"I was very nervous at first to be sure," Margot replied. "After just a short few minutes, though, I was feeling the energy from the spectators and the dance went very well. I could see people in the first few rows tearing up as we danced to the beautiful music, and I was sure that Clem was doing the same. I got to see Clem after the performance, and the first thing he did was embrace me ever so tightly and tell me that he loved me. I could tell by the look in his eyes that he was moved by our performance."

"Did you get to spend any time with him after the performance?" I asked.

Margot replied, "Not much. The Queen Mary was leaving the very next day for Cherbourg, France, and the passengers needed to be back on the ship for a morning departure. Shortly after the performance ended, Rhoda and Clem said their final goodbyes and left the theater. Before he left, Clem told me he was seriously considering staying in England after the airshow for a few weeks before going back to the States. Had I known what was to occur, I would have begged him to stay with me in London. Life doesn't present you with the future; it presents you with the now. You have to do the best you can with the present, with no remorse. That is why I try to never become angry with a person or a situation. I learned a lot from my brief time with Clem, and learned even more after I lost him."

Margot was tearing up again, and I gave her some time to gently wipe her eyes with the white handkerchief she was holding. My tears began to flow as well; we must have looked a sight.

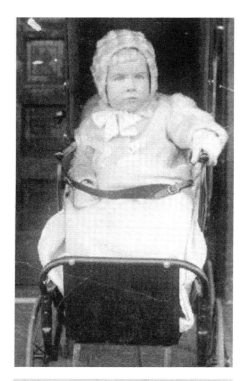

This is among Clem's earliest photos. He's believed to be around two years old.
(Alice Pline)

Clem, on left, and his brother Francis "Lefty."
(Alice Pline)

Gottlieb and Louise Sohn
(Leon Kramer)

Rosalia with Francis "Lefty"
and Clem. (Alice Pline)

The Kramer sisters. Left to right- Maggie Motz, Catherine "Deanie" Kissane, Rosalia Sohn. (Alice Pline)

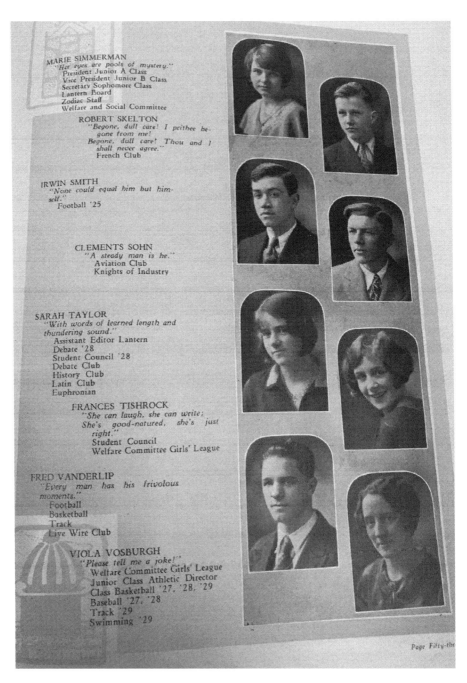

Clem's Lansing Eastern High School picture.
(The Lantern, 1929 Lansing Eastern High School yearbook)

Clem in parachute without wings. (Alice Pline)

Above: Clem with his boss Art Davis (Leon Kramer)

Below and facing page: Clem's amazing wings.
(Dean Feldpausch)

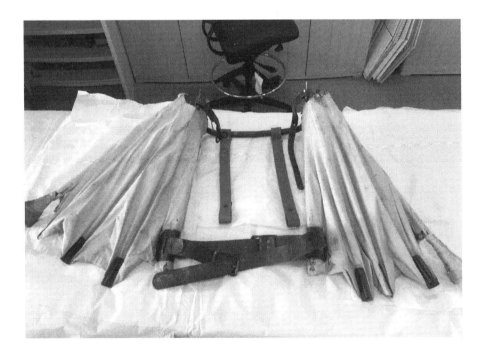

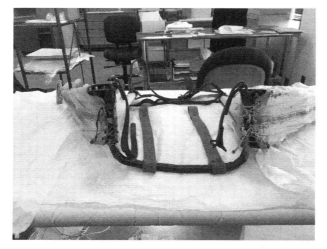

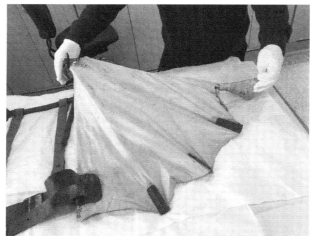

Clem and one of the airplanes he owned.
(Leon Kramer)

Clem preparing to take flight. (Clem Sohn "The Birdman,"
by Cameron Lancaster, Fowler, MI, Village website)

Margot Fonteyn publicity photo. (Wikipedia)

Fonteyn and Helpmann in "The Sleeping Beauty," Sadler's Wells 1950 US tour. (Wikipedia)

French newspaper artist rendition of Clem's final jump.
(La Domenica Del Corriere, *May 9, 1937)*

Here Are Scenes Before and After Tragic Fall of Lansing Batman Fortnight Ago

(Daily News, *New York, New York, June 10, 1934*)

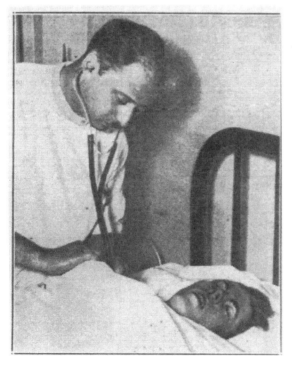

Jerry Wessling who died playing chicken with Clem Sohn. (Daily News, *New York, New York, June 10, 1934*)

CLEMENTS A. SOHN - '30

"THERE ARE SOME PIONEER SOULS WHO BLAZE
THEIR PATHS WHERE HIGHWAYS NEVER RAN"

IN MEMORY OF CLEMENTS A. SOHN WHO GAVE HIS LIFE
IN PARIS, FRANCE APRIL 25, 1937, IT WAS HIS AMBITION
TO PROMOTE AVIATION BY ATTEMPTING AS THE
ORIGINAL BAT WING JUMPER THE PERFECTION OF THIS ART

*Above: A plaque which once was
displayed in Lansing Eastern
High School. Its whereabouts is
no longer known.* (Lansing State
Journal, *May 10, 1937)*

*Left: Clem's headstone in the
Fowler cemetery.
(Dean Feldpausch)*

*Next page: Grave marker given to
Clem's family by a group of French
pilots. Translation: These old
stems for a friend.
(Dean Feldpausch)*

GREATEST FEAR

I wanted to hear the details of what happened next in Clem's life, but I didn't know how to ask Margot about this. She seemed very distraught at this point in our conversation. I don't know if Margot could sense that I wanted to learn more, or if she was simply determined to speak about something that she had held deep inside for so long. Whatever the reason, Margot finally continued to speak about Clem without provocation, only a faint waver in her voice betraying her true emotions.

On Monday, April 19, 1937, Rhoda and Clem were aboard the Queen Mary waiting to embark to Cherbourg. The itinerary called for the ship to leave by 11 a.m., but problems in the Number Four Boiler Room caused the journey to be further delayed. The ship did not leave Southampton until 3 p.m. the next day. As a result, Clem and Rhoda were not able to disembark from the ship in Cherbourg until 10 p.m. Tuesday on the evening of April 20. Clem probably could have asked for preferential treatment and disembarked sooner, but it wasn't in his heart to do such a thing. He gathered his belongings, which included his street clothes, flight suit, batwings, and parachute, and waited patiently in line with the rest of the passengers to leave the ship.

The port in Cherbourg would play an important near-future role in World War II. In a little over three years, France would surrender to Hitler and the Germans would acquire Cherbourg for their own use. During the Battle of Normandy, Cherbourg would be recaptured; in June of 1944, the Germans retreated under Allied pressure but not before destroying most of the port's facilities. It would take Allied forces three months of renovation before the port could be used again on a limited basis. However, on this day Cherbourg was the gateway to France for Rhoda and Clem, and the first leg of their journey to Vincennes.

When they walked down the gangplank and stepped foot on the pier, there were a few French reporters waiting to take some pictures and speak with Clem. Clem took the time to pose for them under the pier lights and give a few brief comments. Clem understood that they would need the pictures and story to hype his arrival and create interest in the airshow.

Clem was told that a driver had been sent to the port at Cherbourg to pick up him and Rhoda for the three hundred seventy-kilometer drive to Vincennes. However, no one appeared at the dock to pick them up. Clem went back onto the ship to find information on where they might stay for the night until they could find the assigned driver the next morning. When the ship's captain heard of their predicament, he was very glad to let them back on board to stay in their cabins one more night. So, Clem and Rhoda gathered their belongings and walked the gangplank back to their cabins. They were both very tired and anxious to get to Vincennes. Clem always liked to be at airshows at least two days ahead of any scheduled jumps so that he could dry and repack his parachutes, as well as speak with the pilot he would be working with. He liked to ride in the plane he would be jumping from to ensure that it provided him the room and safety he needed for a clean jump. This was already Wednesday evening, and he had not yet met his driver for the long trip to Vincennes. Clem was scheduled to take his first jump on Sunday. These things plagued his mind for sure, but more grievous to Clem than that was not seeing Margot. She had become such a regular part of his days for the last nearly two weeks that not seeing her was tugging at his heart.

On Thursday, April 21, at 8 a.m., Rhoda and Clem gathered their belongings once again and carried them down the gangplank to the dock to await their driver. They had no specific contact information for anyone related to the driver, but Rhoda was able to find a telephone at the port station and have the operator contact someone at the venue in Vincennes. The first English-speaking person she talked to did not know who to speak with regarding the driver but vowed to find out and call the station back. Rhoda went back to the driveway entrance of the port to wait with Clem. An hour passed; they both felt increasingly helpless. There was nothing they could really do but wait. A light rain began to fall, and the weary travelers were contemplating what to do with their gear when a white 1934 British Salmson pulled up to them.

"Clem Sohn?" was all that the driver asked as he rolled down the window.

"Yes, that's me," replied a relieved Clem as he walked to the automobile.

The driver got out of the car and opened the petite trunk to place some of the smaller items that Rhoda and Clem brought with them. Then he opened the passenger side rear door and began to shove the remainder of their items in the back seat. The quantity of luggage left virtually no room in the back seat for a passenger, so Rhoda sat in the middle of the front seat between the men as the three of them began the long, slow drive to Vincennes. There was not much room in the seat for the three of them, and they were very much pressed against each other. The automobile was a four-speed with a stick shift on the floor next to Rhoda's left leg. The first time the driver reached down to shift, he touched the calf of Rhoda's leg with the back of his hand, and very much seemed to enjoy this. Rhoda did not appreciate the look on his face after the first time he shifted, but she endured this discomfort until the first time they stopped for gasoline. After that she sat next to the door, with Clem in the middle next to the driver. The driver did not speak English, and neither Rhoda nor Clem spoke French. This made the ride very long and somewhat irritating. In the course of the brief conversation they were able to have, they learned that the driver's name was Gaston. It was too confusing to try to convey anything more, and much of the ride was speechless.

The Salmson they rode in was a twelve-horsepower automobile that had a plain but clean interior. This automobile featured rubber engine mounts, a new innovation that helped to minimize vibration from the engine. It also had an independent suspension, which provided a fairly comfortable ride rolling through the French countryside. The Salmson averaged around thirty-five miles per hour on the long journey. There was a slight odor of exhaust as the car went down the road, which Rhoda reduced significantly by rolling down the passenger-side window slightly. Clem and Rhoda were drifting in and out of sleep as the driver chauffeured them; the sporadic patches of rough and bumpy road and the occasional stops for livestock kept the two from gaining any meaningful, restful sleep.

The threesome stopped in Caen for lunch. The rain they experienced as they were leaving Cherbourg had long dissipated, and there were sunny skies in Caen. They were able to find an open-air restaurant along the main city street and ordered Chicken Marengo with fougasse bread and tea. Legend has it that Chicken Marengo was named for the meal served to Napoleon Bonaparte after his victory at the Battle of Marengo in June of 1800. The chicken-based cuisine became a favorite of the great conqueror Napoleon from that day forward. This meal—along with the fresh air and absence of jouncing—was welcomed by Rhoda, who was beginning to feel a little ill from Gaston's unpredictable driving. After lunch, Clem readjusted the contents of the back seat and was able to place a couple of items on the front seat between the driver and him. Moving these items created enough space for Rhoda to sit in the back seat next to the passenger's side window. This helped ease the tension from the close quarters they'd experienced up to that point. The distance from Cherbourg to Caen was about one hundred twenty-two kilometers; there were still another five hours of driving ahead of them before they completed their journey.

When they finally got to Vincennes, it was 7 p.m. Gaston took them to the Hotel du Château, where rooms had already been reserved for their stay on the second floor. It seemed nice to finally be out of the automobile and inside a hospitable building. Clem and Rhoda were hungry after the second leg of their journey, so they went to the restaurant attached to the hotel and got some sandwiches before going to their rooms for the night. Clem tried calling Margot from the front desk of the hotel, but there was no answer. Clem missed Margot so much that his stomach actually ached for her. Before leaving the lobby, Clem asked for and received a British newspaper, which he took up to his room. The newspaper contained a surprising amount of news from the United States and the rest of the world; much more, it seemed, than American papers typically featured of world events. Among the pages, he found an article about an American horse named Seabiscuit that was making quite a splash in the horse racing world. This horse had been racing for less than two years and had already accumulated seventeen wins. Reading the paper killed some time as he waited for his body to signal it was finally ready for sleep. The London paper was something that reminded him of Margot, and was a welcome distraction. After reading it, he lay on his bed and conjured up memories of the times he'd spent with Margot, falling asleep with her dancing in his mind.

"What were you doing at this time?" I asked Margot.

"When we got back from our trip from New York, the troupe was a little rusty," Margot explained. "We had worked with the New York Symphony Orchestra when we were in the States. When we came back to England, we once again began working with the London Symphony Orchestra. It may seem like music is just music, but when dancing at the level we were dancing at, the slightest variation has an effect on the dance presentation. As a troupe, we spent a lot of time getting reacclimated to our home orchestra and working on new ballet presentations while performing in front of an audience five nights each week. It was quite grueling. I was very miserable during these first few days. I missed Clem so much and was so looking forward to seeing him again after the French airshow. I didn't know where he was staying, and was hoping to speak with him on the Bell telephone."

On Friday, April 23, at 8 a.m., Clem paid a driver to take Rhoda and him to the Hippodrome de Vincennes, which was about two miles south of the center of Vincennes. The venue was originally built in 1863 as a horse-racing track, and had a rich tradition of entertaining crowds with varied events. It had a long, straight section of track that was three thousand meters long, which was perfect for an airplane runway. It also had an adjacent oval track and grandstands, which had a capacity for crowds of up to sixty thousand people. This was all set on an expansive piece of land over one hundred sixty acres in size.

On this day, it was raining slightly. When Rhoda and Clem arrived at the Hippodrome, they found no airplanes on the ground and no pilots in sight. It seemed that rain had plagued them at nearly every turn since they left New York. They made their way to offices in the grandstand area and were able to locate an English-speaking gentleman who directed them to the department for event planning. Inside, they asked for Henry Baudoux, who was the person that Rhoda had communicated with by letter to arrange for Clem to jump at the airshow. They were directed to an elderly Frenchman who spoke fluent English.

"Are you Henry?" Rhoda asked, holding out her hand for a handshake.

"Yes, I am," Henry responded. Grabbing her hand, he brought it up to his face and kissed it.

Rhoda frowned as she tugged her hand back, unused to this sort of greeting. "I'm Rhoda Davis, and this is Clem Sohn," she said, motioning to Clem standing behind her.

"I'm pleased to meet you," Clem said as he shook Henry's out-stretched hand.

"I suppose you are here for your payment?" Henry asked.

"Yes, we are," Rhoda responded. "Clem would also like to speak with the pilot who will be taking him up, if that's possible."

"I do not have any information on who has been selected," Henry said. "I have a contract for you to sign, and an envelope with ten thousand dollars in American currency, just as you requested. We are very excited to have you perform here," the old man added, looking Clem over appraisingly.

"I am looking forward to a wonderful time," Clem replied.

Rhoda quickly read the one-page contract and signed the bottom. She noted that there was also a place for Clem to sign, so she motioned for Clem to place his signature as well. Clem and Rhoda then walked to the track area, leaned on the audience fence, and looked up into the sky, which was overcast but temporarily devoid of rain.

"Will this really be your last show?" Rhoda asked Clem.

"I think so, Rhoda. I'm already looking beyond it. I just want to get back to England to see Margot," Clem replied while looking up into the heavens.

"I can't imagine you not flying and skydiving. It seems that's all you've wanted to do as long as I've known you," Rhoda said.

"I know it seems a little crazy, even for me ... all I can say is I've never felt this way about anyone in my life. If Margot and I can't be together, then what will I have? I'll tell you—just another show, and then another, and another." Clem inhaled deeply, exhaled, his eyes fixed firmly on the bruise-colored sky. "It has to end sometime, Rhoda. Here in France is where it might as well happen."

"Clem would never understand just how true his words would prove," Margot recalled. "The next day was Saturday, the day before he was scheduled to perform. The skies had turned sunny, and the weather forecast for Sunday was very promising. Ticket sales for the airshow were brisk, and it looked like there might be a capacity crowd in attendance."

"Was Clem ever able to speak with you again?" I asked.

"Rhoda wrote me that Clem had tried to call me several times," Margot responded. "Mum wasn't at home due to helping out with the spring cleaning of our church. Meanwhile, I was at the theater working on a new production choreographed by Frederick Ashton. I didn't know where to call Clem, and his calls to our house went unanswered. However, I did receive word from him in a very special way on Saturday night, the eve of his final jump. You remember that Clem and Rhoda left after my show the Sunday prior to board the Queen Mary? Unbeknownst to me, they made a stop before going to the pier.

"On Saturday, April 24th, after our performance at the Sadler's Wells Theatre, the dance troupe met with the patrons and audience, as was our custom. When this visitation was completed, I went back to my dressing room to clean up and slip into my street clothes before heading home. In my room, on the top of my credenza, was a small bouquet of periwinkle flowers with an envelope that had my name, *Margot,* written on it. I picked up the bouquet and smelled the fragrance of the fresh flowers. I could not think of who might have sent them, but my mind was on Clem, and it was nice to have this small bouquet to help me think of him. When I opened the envelope, I found a card that read: *I don't want to be a batman anymore, I wish I was a ballerina like you. Clem.*"

Margot paused in her recounting, tears swimming in her downcast eyes. "Periwinkle has been my very favorite color ever since that day," she said through a sniffle. "Clem understood timing; to him, timing was everything. Rhoda wrote me later that after we last saw each other that Sunday night, he made a stop at a floral shop he spotted on their way to the docks. He bought the flowers and wrote the card, leaving strict instructions for them to be delivered on the night before his performance in France. Such an overwhelmingly beautiful gesture … I wanted desperately to tell him how thankful I was, but I would never see my dear, dear Clem again."

Sunday morning, April 25, 1937, brought a great deal of excitement to Vincennes, France. People from all over Europe were making their way to the Hippodrome de Vincennes to see European pilots from many different countries perform death-defying feats. The grandstands were not filled to capacity as was hoped, but in excess of forty thousand enthusiastic people had come for the festivities. There was one American who would be a key part of the show: the batman, Clem Sohn.

Rhoda and Clem had a driver take them to the straight airstrip, which was about one-quarter mile west of the grandstands. They were told Clem would be able to meet with the pilot at that time and finally see the plane he would jump from. They did not expect a crowd to be in this area, but when they got there, it was evident word had gotten out. There were about three thousand people standing next to the runway, waiting for Clem to arrive.

Clem had opened his parachute bags for both his primary and secondary chutes to let in dry air but had not taken them out completely to ensure they were dry and to repack them. He was planning to do this at the airshow before his jump, but the crowd was so large and so near, there wasn't sufficient space available. Clem could probably have demanded that an area be cleared to take care of this important task, but it was not in his character to give such an order. He knew now he should have aired out his chutes the night before, but he had attended a dinner honoring the performers of the airshow that had lasted long into the evening. He had also tried to contact Margot by telephone, but the calls went unanswered.

When Clem and Rhoda walked from their driver's car to the runway, they were met by a throng of people shouting and cheering for America's batman. A reporter with a loud speaker started asking Clem questions for the benefit of the crowd, his booming French-accented voice interspersed with occasional electronic crackles.

"Mr. Sohn, we are so happy to have you here," the announcer stated into a large microphone. "Can you tell us about your jump today?"

"I'll be performing four jumps today, one every hour from 1 to 4," Clem replied. "I'm planning to jump from an altitude of ten thousand feet, which is about three kilometers."

"How many times have you parachuted?" continued the announcer.

"I've made between two hundred to three hundred jumps," Clem responded.

"What frightens you the most about falling through the air?" the announcer pressed further.

"I feel very much at home in the sky. I feel safer there than in my grandmother's kitchen," Clem said with a smile.

"Good luck, sir," finished the announcer.

At this, Clem walked over to the car that had brought him to the airstrip. He withdrew three canvas bags containing his flight suit, parachutes, and wings, and set them on the ground.

"Do you want to go to the grandstands?" Clem asked of Rhoda.

"Yes, I do," she replied.

"Hop in the car, then, and take it there. I'll look for you at the main gate when I'm finished today," Clem said.

Clem removed the contents of the bags and placed them back into the car. He gave Rhoda a hug, and she departed for the grand-stands. The crowd was amazed as Clem began putting on his gear in preparation for his first jump. After donning his flight suit, Clem opened the bag that contained his primary parachute and stuck his hand inside. The chute felt dry, which gave Clem confidence that the parachute would deploy properly. He strapped on his primary and secondary parachutes, then picked up his wings and carefully belted the metal cage around his torso. He grabbed the paddles of the wings and opened them for the admiring crowd to see. The onlookers met this with a conversational buzz; they had never seen anything so odd or amazing before.

A Curtiss A-12 was the airplane selected for Clem's jump. It was an open two-seated aircraft with the pilot seat in front and a passenger seat behind it, where Clem would sit. The airplane could be flown from either seat, as both control sticks were connected, but Clem did not plan to confuse the pilot by taking control of the plane. The pilot was standing on the ground next to the aircraft. Clem went over to speak with him and quickly learned that he could speak no English. This did not please Clem, as he wanted to be able to communicate if anything seemed irregular during the flight. These issues would normally have been dealt with by bringing in another pilot, but in this case, Clem didn't want to argue. He knew that the pilot had been briefed on the altitude and location in which to fly for his successful flight, so he decided to just let the situation play out. He felt in his heart that this would be his last airshow, so he overlooked these potential problems and simply anticipated completing his four jumps and leaving France for England and Margot.

At the appointed time, Clem climbed a stepladder set next to the back seat of the aircraft, carefully stepping inside. His flight gear was a little bulky, and he had to take care to position himself in the seat without damaging any part of his batwing apparatus. Once Clem was in position and comfortable with his surroundings, he looked at the pilot and nodded that he was ready. The pilot climbed onto the wing and into the front seat, starting up the engine. At this, the crowd began to dispersing toward the grandstands to watch Clem's flight. As Clem's aircraft taxied to the runway, other aircraft were taking off to begin their aerial displays in front of the crowd.

Clem's plane arrived at the southern end of the airstrip and waited for several planes in front to clear the runway. When the conditions appeared right, the pilot revved the engines and made a clean takeoff into the sunny French skies. It would take a few minutes for the plane to reach the appropriate altitude and position for Clem's jump; as he gained in elevation, Clem began mentally preparing for his performance. He visualized jumping from the plane, drifting through the air, and pulling his ripcord at about one thousand feet. After that visualization, he began to wonder what

Margot was doing. He wished so much that she could be there to see him perform as he had seen her.

"What were you doing during Clem's jump?" I asked Margot.

"We had a matinee performance scheduled on that Sunday at the Sadler's Wells Theatre," Margot replied. "I was very nervous thinking about Clem, and wished I was at his side. I remember thinking before the show opened that something might go wrong with his jump. I could not put my finger on it, but I did not dance well that day. I was not able to focus. At one point during my dance, I felt for a second that Clem was calling out to me, and I immediately felt so lonely. I tried to tell my mind that everything was alright, but my heart was telling me something quite different."

When Clem's airplane reached the appropriate spot for his jump, the pilot raised his hand and gave Clem a thumbs-up signal. This was always the most difficult portion of Clem's jumps; disembarking from the plane was far more dangerous than the fall itself, and it was a part of his performance the audience could never see.

Clem rose and cleared the sides of the airplane with his wings. He then stood on the seat while holding onto the airplane's body. When he felt the time was right, he raised his foot over the fuselage and onto a small step on the side of the plane. He then let go of his hold and lunged to the right, safely avoiding the plane's metal frame. He freely fell for about ten seconds with his arms held tightly to his sides and his legs kept together. Then he gripped the paddles of his wings and slowly opened the wing on his right side. Once his right wing was open, he slowly opened the wing on his left side. When his wings were outstretched and he was stable in the sky, he slowly spread his legs to open the rudder of his outfit. When this operation was completed and Clem felt steady, he began making slight variations to his flight by bending his knees and changing the degree of openness of his wings. It did not take much movement in these positions to change directions.

Clem was truly enjoying this flight. He felt so majestic in the air, and he quickly remembered why he was so drawn to this career. Clem began to think Rhoda might be right about him not being able to give up what brought him so much pleasure.

Clem looked out over the French countryside and the crowd below. It was indeed a beautiful sight. Clem swooped and turned as he made his way toward the ground. He began to hear the dim, thin exaltation of the crowd and felt proud to be giving them so much pleasure. As he neared the point of pulling his ripcord, he suddenly thought that maybe Margot needed to see him perform at least once before he hastily decided not to do this anymore.

The time had arrived for Clem to pull his ripcord on his primary parachute, and pull he did. His parachute left its bag and dragged up into the air. A parachutist's greatest fear is that his chute will not open, and that is exactly what happened. Clem received an immediate shot of adrenaline, and he pulled the ripcord on his secondary parachute. But that chute did not come out of its bag. In a last-ditch effort for survival, Clem reached for the lines of his primary chute and tried to spread them so that the air would open it, but nothing worked … Clem was doomed.

In the few seconds Clem had remaining in his life, his mind came alive with daydream scenes. Time seemed to move very, very slowly; in spite of the fact that he was desperately pulling on the lines of his parachute, he began seeing his mother Rosalia on her deathbed holding her bloodstained handkerchief. He felt a wave of raw grief at this scene, his heart breaking anew over his mother's long-ago death. He then saw Margot dancing brilliantly on stage.

His mind's eye took him to Margot as she laughed sweetly on the swing in Mecklenburgh Square. He saw the look in her eyes as they embraced so lovingly. He imagined her smiling at him from the front yard of a house with a large back porch in a country setting. She wore a beautiful periwinkle dress, and two small children were holding her hands. He saw his father Gottlieb shaking his finger at him, telling him in remonstrating tones that skydiving would eventually kill him. His father had told him this many times, but Clem's pride would not let him listen. Clem saw his brother Lefty throwing a wide curveball to him. Clem loved being with Lefty, and when the pitch struck his mitt in the center of the strike zone, he jumped for joy. Other images flashed by quickly in his mind, a brief lifetime of daring experience. And then suddenly—all was gone.

Clem had fallen at a rate of nearly two hundred miles per hour; he died instantly upon hitting the ground. People in the audience would say that the impact of Clem's body sounded like a small explosion. Clem left a depression in the ground almost two feet deep—the coroner later wrote that every bone in his body had been broken. Rhoda fainted at the sight of Clem's landing and was not easily revived. When she finally did come around, she tried to go to Clem's side. Unfortunately, about one thousand people had left the stands and tried to do the same thing. Rhoda could not get close, and she would not see his body and the gruesome effects of his fall until the next day, when she arranged for his remains to return to the United States.

Margot began to weep as she relayed these final moments of Clem's life. I wept as well. Finally, Margot spoke.

"It was very fortunate that I had exchanged addresses with Clem and Rhoda before they left for France. One month after Clem passed, I received a long letter from Rhoda telling me about Clem's final moments on this earth. She knew I would want to know everything about this terrible tragedy. We wrote each other several times in that first year after Clem left us. I had an overwhelming feeling that Clem's preoccupation with our relationship had played some kind of role in his death. For all these years, I haven't told anyone about our love. In fact, I told people that I'd never met him. But I suppose it is time to finally set the record straight."

WINGS OF GRANDEUR

Tere was nothing I could say to Margot at this point. All I could do was grieve with her. I turned to look at Clem's gravestone. The wings at the top of his stone had looked like bird's wings when I first saw them, but now they looked like wings of grandeur.

"It took a long time for me to get over the death of my love, Clem Sohn," Margot continued after collecting herself. "In a way, I am happy for him, because he is finally with his mother. He's no doubt learned what she wanted him to know on her deathbed. I read every news article I could find about Clem after he left me, and there were many. I learned most of the details of his death from them. Newspapers from all over the world wrote about him for about a week, and then the German Hindenburg dirigible accident occurred, and that story consumed the newspapers. My life went on despite Clem's abrupt departure from it. In the fall of 1937, the year Clem died, I would meet the man I would eventually marry. However, I did not marry him until eighteen years later. I could not bring myself to marry him sooner, though he wanted that badly. I had to say goodbye to Clem in my own private way, and he will always have a special, sacred place in my heart."

I was watching Margot stare at Clem's tombstone, my own vision still clouded by tears, when suddenly I caught movement out of the corner of my eye. Automobiles began to arrive at the cemetery, almost two dozen of them; people got out and started walking toward Clem's gravesite.

"What is this?" Margot asked, in some alarm.

"There's going to be a ceremony today in honor of Clem," I responded. "I need to go over and take some pictures. Do you mind?"

"Of course not, Ren, please do what you have to do," came Margot's reply.

I left my notepad and shoulder bag near Margot and picked up my camera. Walking toward the commotion, I began taking pictures and speaking with the first arrivals; this assignment had taken on a whole new meaning to me, and I wanted to gather as much information as I could. Perhaps I could send some of my photos to my new friend Margot.

After several minutes of picture-taking and interviews, a wreath unexpectedly fell from the sky onto the far east side of the cemetery grounds, where no gravesites were located. Then another fell … followed by another and many more. I looked up into the sky and noted a lone airplane circling the cemetery, leaving those beautiful accolades. I ran to the nearest wreath, picked it up, and started toward the little iron bench where Margot was seated. I felt that she should have one of these mementos from this special day. However, when I approached the bench, Margot was not there. I looked toward her vehicle and saw it slowly, unobtrusively leaving the cemetery.

I paused for a moment and thought about our conversation as Margot's automobile slowly drove out of sight. I realized that her premature departure was the action of a person deeply in love. Margot did not want to take any attention away from what was meant to be Clem's day—Clem would have reacted in a similar fashion if he was here and this was a celebration of Margot's life. Clem and Margot were the best in the world at what they did, yet they were honest, humble, and loving individuals in spite of their successes. They always seemed to put the needs of others ahead of their own.

I feel like I learned something very valuable from Margot on that day. I had been feeling sorry for myself, because I wasn't receiving the breaks I thought I deserved as a budding journalist. Was it breaks I should be looking for? Maybe I should concentrate on being the best I could be at my craft and let the love of my career be my happiness. Margot and Clem took years to develop into the consummate professionals they turned out to be: They understood the value of hard work and a focus on their life's ambitions. Maybe it was time I do the same.

I went to the library and did research on Margot Fonteyn while working up my article. I was fascinated to learn many remarkable facts about her life that she had not shared with me. Margot was indeed a renowned ballerina. She danced throughout the World War II conflict, even as the Germans were bombing London. Her performances were so gripping that people refused to leave the theater even as the bomb sirens blared. She danced all over the world in beautiful productions, such as *Swan Lake, Nutcracker, Sleeping Beauty, Giselle, The Wanderer, Hamlet*, and many more. She would make several visits to the United States to showcase her amazing talent.

Margot eventually married Tito Arias, a high-ranking official from Panama. She wined and dined with some of the richest and most important entertainers and politicians of her time. Tito was involved in an attempted overthrow of the Panamanian government, and by association so was Margot. She was even jailed for a brief period. Tito was eventually paralyzed by a bullet from an assassination attempt, and Margot cared for him until he died several decades later (he was still alive when we met that day in

April 1987). Through it all, she remained a classy and inspirational woman and performer. I am forever grateful that I had the opportunity to meet such a wonderful person.

The story I began writing on that day turned out amazing, thanks to Margot. I had limits on the length of the article, so I had to be concise, but I think I wrote a tale that would have pleased both Clem and Margot. I never heard from Margot again and am unsure if she ever read what I had written. Several weeks went by after my news article was published. I received many compliments on the content and quality of the story. The editor of the *Clinton County News* even gave me a raise, largely the result of this work.

I cannot ever thank Margot enough for the time she spent with me, and for the effect she had on my life. I will forever be in awe of the too-brief love she shared with America's greatest aerial batman, Clem Sohn.

ACKNOWLEDGEMENTS

First and foremost I want to thank my in-laws Erwin & Alice Pline. It is through them that I am related to the amazing Clem Sohn. Alice was also able to give me first-hand information regarding some life events of Clem Sohn.

Next I want to thank my wife Marcia, my daughters, and their families. They provide me with a loving environment in which to live my life. They help to keep me sane in a crazy world.

I also want to thank my book editors, Karen Crosby, Scott Couturier, and Doug Weaver. This is my first attempt at book writing, and they have helped me greatly with their excellent advice. A thanks also goes out to Heather Shaw for her work on the text format and photo inserts, Tajín Robles for the cover illustration, and Matthew Mitchell for the author portrait.

Finally I want to thank my high school composition teacher, the late Dennis Pilmore. His advice to his students was instrumental in giving me confidence to proceed with this project. He used to say, "It doesn't matter what you write, just write something every day." He encouraged journal writing as a way to keep the pen to paper and develop good writing skills.

DEAN R. FELDPAUSCH was born in September of 1955 in St. Johns Michigan. He is married to Marcia, and has three daughters; Kendall, Gwen, and Laura. He has held job positions in housing construction, tax auditing, and IT management, for several companies in Michigan. Dean has earned a Bachelor's degree from Northwood University, and a Master's degree from Central Michigan University. Dean was a wedding singer for many years, and has performed in over twenty stage productions with local theatre groups. *The Batman and the Ballerina* is his first published literary work.

Made in the USA
Middletown, DE
29 October 2018